PEDRO PÁRAMO

JUAN RULFO

WITH A FOREWORD BY
GABRIEL GARCÍA MÁRQUEZ

TRANSLATED BY
DOUGLAS J. WEATHERFORD

Grove Press
New York

Originally published in Mexico in 1955 by Fondo de Cultura Económica.

Published simultaneously in Canada
Printed in Canada

This book was set in 11-pt. Berkeley Oldstyle
by Alpha Design & Composition of Pittsfield, NH.

First Grove Atlantic paperback edition: November 2023

Library of Congress Cataloging-in-Publication data is available for this title.

ISBN 978-0-8021-6093-5
eISBN 978-0-8021-6106-2

Grove Press
an imprint of Grove Atlantic
154 West 14th Street
New York, NY 10011

Distributed by Publishers Group West

groveatlantic.com

23 24 25 26   10 9 8 7 6 5 4 3 2 1

PEDRO PÁRAMO

Also by Juan Rulfo

The Burning Plain
The Golden Cockerel & Other Writings

. . . .
CONTENTS

FOREWORD

by Gabriel García Márquez

Translated by N. J. Sheerin

My discovery of Juan Rulfo—like that of Kafka—will without doubt be an essential chapter in my memoirs. I had arrived in Mexico on the same day Ernest Hemingway pulled the trigger—June 2, 1961—and not only had I not read Juan Rulfo's books, I hadn't even heard of him. It was very strange: first of all because in those days I kept up to date with the latest goings-on in the literary world, and even more so when it came to Latin American novels; secondly because the first people I got in touch with in Mexico were the writers who worked with Manuel Barbachano Ponce[1] in his Dracula's Castle on the streets of Córdoba, and the editors of the literary magazine *Novedades*, headed up by Fernando Benítez.[2] Naturally, they

---

1. Manuel Barbachano Ponce (1925–1994): A highly influential Mexican producer, most notably of Luís Buñuel's *Nazarín*, he was also a director and screenwriter in his own right. Five years after García Márquez's arrival in Mexico, Barbachano Ponce would produce Carlos Velo's film adaptation of *Pedro Páramo*.

2. Fernando Benítez Gutiérrez (1912–2000): Widely admired Mexican writer, editor, and anthropologist. A champion of Mexico's Indigenous population, he is best remembered for his four-volume work *Los indios de México* (*Indians of Mexico*). Benítez was also famously generous and gave early advice to writers such as Elena Poniatowska, Carlos Monsiváis, and José Emilio Pacheco.

all knew Juan Rulfo well. Yet it was at least six months before anyone mentioned him to me. Perhaps because Juan Rulfo, contrary to what happens with most great authors, is a writer who is much read but little spoken of.

I lived in an apartment without an elevator on calle Renán in the Anzures neighborhood of Mexico City with Mercedes and Rodrigo, who was less than two years old at the time. There was a double mattress on the floor of the master bedroom, a crib in the other room, and a kitchen table which doubled as a writing desk in the living room, with two single-seat chairs which were put to whatever use was needed. We had decided to stay in this city which at that time still retained a human scale, with its diaphanous air and deliriously colored flowers in the avenues, but the immigration authorities didn't seem inclined to share in our happiness. Half our lives were spent in immobile queues, sometimes in the rain, in the penitents' courtyards of the Secretariat of the Interior. In my free hours I wrote notes on Colombian literature which I read out live on air for Radio Universidad, then under the auspices of Max Aub.[3] These notes were so honest that one day the Colombian ambassador phoned the broadcaster to lodge a formal complaint. According to him, mine were not notes on Colombian literature, but against Colombian literature. Max Aub called me to his office, and that, I thought, was the end of the only means of income I had managed to secure in six months. In fact, precisely the opposite happened.

—I haven't had time to listen to the program—Max Aub told me—but if it's as your ambassador says, then it must be very good.

---

3. Max Aub Mohrenwitz (1903–1972): Spanish-Mexican writer who lived in Mexico in exile from Franco's Spain. A friend of André Malraux, he is most famous for the cycle of novels "El laberinto mágico," set during the Spanish Civil War.

I was thirty-two years old, had in Colombia an ephemeral journalistic career, had just spent three very useful and difficult years in Paris and eight months in New York, and wanted to write screenplays in Mexico. The Mexican writing community at that time was similar to Colombia's, and I felt very much at home there. Six years earlier I had published my first novel, *Leaf Storm*, and I had three unpublished books: *No One Writes to the Colonel*, which appeared around that time in Colombia; *In Evil Hour*, which was published by the publishing house Editorial Era shortly afterwards on the recommendation of Vicente Rojo,[4] and the story collection *Big Mama's Funeral*. Of this last I had only incomplete drafts, since Álvaro Mutis[5] had lent the originals to our much-loved Elena Poniatowska[6] before my arrival in Mexico, and she had lost them. Later I managed to reconstruct the stories, and Sergio Galindo[7] published them at the University of Veracruz on the recommendation of Álvaro Mutis.

So I was already a writer with five underground books. For me that wasn't a problem, since neither then nor ever have I written for fame, but rather so that my friends would love me

4. Vicente Rojo Almazán (1932–): A Barcelona-born Spanish-Mexican artist and member of Mexico's so-called Generación de la Ruptura (Breakaway Generation), he cofounded Editorial Era and would design the original cover to *One Hundred Years of Solitude*.

5. Álvaro Mutis Jaramillo (1923–2013): A Colombian poet, novelist, and essayist, and winner of the 2002 Neustadt Prize for Literature, his most famous work in English remains *The Adventures and Misadventures of Maqroll*. He was a close friend of García Márquez, who called him "one of the greatest writers of our time."

6. Elena Poniatowska (1932–): French-Mexican novelist and journalist, and winner of the 2013 Cervantes Prize. Her works in English include *Massacre in Mexico*, an investigation into the 1968 Tlatelolco massacre, and *Leonora*, a biography of British-Mexican artist Leonora Carrington.

7. Sergio Galindo Márquez (1926–1993): Mexican novelist and short-story writer, erstwhile director of the Mexican Institute for Fine Arts, member of the Spanish Royal Academy, and honorary OBE.

more, and I believed I had managed that. My great problem as a novelist was that after those books I felt I had driven myself up a blind alley, and I was looking everywhere for an escape route. I was well acquainted with good authors and bad authors alike who could have shown me the way out, and yet I felt myself going around and around in concentric circles. I didn't see myself as spent. On the contrary: I felt I still had many novels in me, but I couldn't conceive of a convincing and poetic way of writing them. That is where I was when Álvaro Mutis climbed with great strides the seven stories up to my apartment with a bundle of books, extracted from this mountain the smallest and shortest, and said as he laughed himself to death:

—Read this shit and learn!

The book was *Pedro Páramo*.

That night I couldn't sleep until I had read it twice. Not since the awesome night I read Kafka's *Metamorphosis* in a down-at-the-heels student boardinghouse in Bogotá—almost ten years earlier—had I been so overcome. The next day I read *The Burning Plain*, and my astonishment remained intact. Much later, in a doctor's waiting room, I came across a medical journal with another of Rulfo's scattered masterpieces: "The Legacy of Matilde Arcángel." The rest of that year I couldn't read a single other author, because they all seemed inferior.

I still hadn't escaped my bedazzlement when someone told Carlos Velo that I could recite from memory whole passages of *Pedro Páramo*. The truth went even further: I could recite the entire book front to back and vice versa without a single appreciable error, I could tell you on which page of my edition each scene could be found, and there wasn't a single aspect of its characters' personalities which I wasn't deeply familiar with.

Carlos Velo entrusted me with the adaptation for cinema of another of Juan Rulfo's stories, the only one which I hadn't yet read: "The Golden Cockerel." There were sixteen pages of it, very crumpled, typed on disintegrating tissue paper by three different typewriters. Even if they hadn't told me who it was by, I would have known straightaway. The language wasn't as intricate as the rest of Juan Rulfo's work, and there were very few of his usual literary devices on show, but his guardian angel flew about every aspect of the writing. Later, Carlos Velo and Carlos Fuentes asked me to read and critique their screenplay for a film adaptation—the first—of *Pedro Páramo*.

I mention these two jobs—the results of which were a long way from being any good—because they obliged me to dive even further into a novel which without doubt I knew better than even its own author (who, by the by, I didn't meet until several years later). Carlos Velo had done something striking: he had cut up the temporal fragments of *Pedro Páramo*, and had reassembled the plot in strictly chronological order. As a straightforward resource to work from it seemed legitimate, although the resulting text was vastly different from the original: flat and disjointed. But it was a useful exercise for me in understanding Juan Rulfo's secret carpentry, and very revealing of his rare wisdom.

There were two fundamental problems with adapting *Pedro Páramo* for screen. The first was the question of names. As subjective as it sounds, in some way every name resembles the person who bears it, and this is something that is much more obvious in fiction than in real life. Juan Rulfo has said—or is claimed to have said—that he takes his characters' names from the headstones of the graves in cemeteries throughout Jalisco. The only thing we can be certain of is that there are no proper nouns as proper—which is to say, as appropriate—as those borne by the characters in his books. It seemed impossible to me—indeed, it still seems impossible—that an actor could ever be found who would perfectly suit the name of the character he was to play.

The other problem—inseparable from the first—was that of age. Throughout his work, Juan Rulfo has been careful to take very little care with the lifespans of his creations. The critic Narciso Costa Ros recently made a fascinating attempt to establish them in *Pedro Páramo*. I had always thought, purely through poetic intuition, that when Pedro Páramo finally takes Susana San Juan to the Media Luna, his vast domain, she is already sixty-two years old. Pedro Páramo must be around five years her senior. In fact, the whole tragedy seems much greater, much more terrible and beautiful, if the precipitous passion that sets it in motion is so geriatric as to offer no real relief. Such a great and poetic feat would be unthinkable in the cinema. In those darkened theatres, the love lives of the elderly don't move anyone.

The difficult thing about looking at things in this lovely, deliberate way is that poetic sense does not always tally with common sense. The month in which certain scenes occur is essential in any analysis of Juan Rulfo's work, something I doubt he was even conscious of. In poetic works—and *Pedro Páramo* is a poetic work of the highest order—authors often invoke the months of the year for reasons outside strict chronology. What's more: in many cases an author may change the name of the month, day, or even year solely to avoid an infelicitous rhyme, or some disharmony, without recognizing that these changes can cause a critic to reach an insurmountable conclusion about the work in question. This is the case not just with days and months, but with flowers too. There are writers who use them purely for the sophistication of their names, without paying much attention to whether they correspond to the place or season. This is why it is not uncommon to find books where geraniums flower on the beach and tulips in the snow. In *Pedro Páramo*, where it is impossible to be entirely sure where the line between the living and the dead is drawn, any precision is all the more unattainable. No one can know, of course, how many years death may last.

I wanted to write all this to say that my profound exploration of Juan Rulfo's work was what finally showed me the way to continue with my writing, and for that reason it would be impossible for me to write about him without it seeming that I'm writing about myself. I also want to say that I read it all again before writing these brief reminiscences, and that once again I am the helpless victim of the same astonishment that struck me the first time around. They number scarcely more than three hundred pages, but they are as great—and, I believe, as enduring—as those of Sophocles.

I CAME TO COMALA because I was told my father lived here, a man named Pedro Páramo. That's what my mother told me. And I promised her I'd come see him as soon as she died. I squeezed her hands as a sign I would. After all, she was near death, and I was of a mind to promise her anything. "Don't fail to visit him —she urged—. Some call him one thing, some another. I'm sure he'd love to meet you." That's why I couldn't refuse her, and after agreeing so many times I just kept at it until I had to struggle to free my hands from hers, which were now without life.

Before this she had told me:

—Don't ask him for anything. Just insist on what's ours. What he was obligated to give me but never did . . . Make him pay dearly, my son, for the indifference he showed toward us.

—I will, Mother.

I never thought I'd keep my promise. Until recently when I began to imagine all kinds of possibilities and allowed my fantasies to run free. And that's how a whole new world started swirling around in my head, a world built on expectations I had for that man named Pedro Páramo, my mother's husband. That's why I came to Comala.

IT WAS DURING the dog days of summer, when the August winds blow hot, tainted by the rotting smell of saponaria flowers.

The road rose and fell: *"It rises or falls according to whether one's going or coming. For the person who's leaving, it rises; for the one who's coming, it falls."*

—What did you say was the name of that town down there?

—Comala, señor.

—You sure we've already made it to Comala?

—I'm sure, señor.

—And why does it look so sad?

—It's the times, señor.

I had imagined I'd see the place of my mother's memories, of her nostalgia, a nostalgia of tattered sighs. She was always sighing, mourning the loss of Comala, hoping to return. But she never came back. Now I've come in her place. And I come bearing the same eyes with which she saw these things, because she gave me her eyes to see: *"There, just beyond Los Colimotes pass, you'll find a beautiful view of a green plain, with a bit of yellow from the ripening corn. From that spot you'll see Comala, turning the land white, lighting it up at night."* And her voice was secretive, almost without sound, as if she were speaking to herself . . . My mother.

—And why are you headed to Comala, if I might ask? —I heard someone say.

—I'm going to see my father —I answered.

—Ah! —he said.

And we returned to our silence.

We walked downhill, listening to the cadent trotting of the burros. Our eyes swelling with fatigue in the intense August heat.

—He's gonna throw you quite the party —I heard again from the voice of the man walking alongside me—. He'll be glad to see someone after so many years with no one passing through.

Later he added:

—Whoever you are, he'll be happy to see you.

The plain resembled a translucent pool in the pulsing heat of the sun, dissipating in the distance where a gray horizon took shape. And beyond that, a line of mountains. And even farther still, a never-ending distance.

—And what's your father like, if I might ask?

—I don't know him —I said—. I just know his name is Pedro Páramo.

—Ah! You don't say.

—That's the name I was given.

I again heard the "ah!" of the muleteer.

I had met up with him at Los Encuentros, where several roads came together. I was there waiting, until finally this guy showed up.

—Where you headed? —I asked.

—Down that way, señor.

—You familiar with a place called Comala?

—That's where I'm going.

So I followed him. I walked behind trying to match his pace, until he seemed to notice I was following and slowed his stride. After that we walked side by side so close together our shoulders were almost touching.

—I'm also one of Pedro Páramo's sons —he told me.

A flock of crows passed overhead through an empty sky, crying caw, caw, caw.

After dropping down out of the hills, we descended even farther. We had left the hot air above and were now sinking into a pure heat that had no air. Everything seemed to be waiting for something.

—It's hot here —I said.

—It is, but this is nothing —responded the other guy—. Try to relax. You'll feel it worse when we get to Comala. That place sits on the burning embers of the earth, at the very mouth of

Hell. They say many of those who die there and go to Hell come back to fetch their blankets.

—Do you know Pedro Páramo? —I asked.

I dared pose the question because I saw a hint of understanding in his eyes.

—Who is he? —I inquired again.

—Bitterness incarnate —he answered.

He took a swat at the burros, without any need to do so, since they were well ahead of us and focused on the descent.

I felt my mother's portrait tucked away in my shirt pocket, keeping my heart warm, as if she too were sweating. It was an old photograph, worn along the edges; but it was the only one I'd ever seen of her. I had found it in the kitchen cabinet, in a clay pot full of herbs: lemon balm leaves, castilla blossoms, twigs of rue. I've kept it ever since. It was the only one. My mother was always opposed to being photographed. She said portraits were a form of witchcraft. And it seemed she was right, because hers was full of holes, like pinpricks, with one large enough to fit your middle finger through located right where her heart should be.

It's the same photograph I have with me here, hoping it might help my father recognize me.

—Look at this —the muleteer says as he comes to a halt—. See that hill over there, the one that looks like a pig's bladder? Well, just beyond that is the Media Luna. Now turn that way. You see the top of that hill? Look at it. Now turn and look this way. See that other hilltop you can barely make out for being so far away? Well, that's the Media Luna from one end to the other. As they say, every bit of land as far as the eye can see. And all that ground is his. The thing is, our mothers pushed us into this miserable world laid out on the ground on petates even though we were sons of Pedro Páramo. And the funniest part is he's the one who took us to be baptized. That's got to be what happened to you too, right?

—I don't recall.

—The hell you say!

—What's that?

—I said we're almost there, señor.

—I can see that. But what came through here?

—A roadrunner, señor. That's what they call those birds.

—No, I was asking about the town. It seems so alone, as if abandoned. As if no one were living here.

—It doesn't just seem that way. That's how it is. Nobody lives here.

—And Pedro Páramo?

—Pedro Páramo died years ago.

IT WAS THE TIME of day when children in small towns everywhere play in the streets, filling the afternoon with their shouting. When the black walls still reflect the yellow light of the sun.

At least that's what I'd seen in Sayula, just yesterday at this same hour. And I'd seen the still air shattered by doves flapping their wings as if they were breaking free of the day. They flew about, dipping toward the rooftops as the shouts of children fluttered about and seemed to turn blue in the evening sky.

Now here I was, in this town devoid of all sound. I heard my footsteps as they fell on the rounded stones that paved the streets. Hollow footsteps, echoing off walls tinged by the light of the setting sun.

That was the time of day when I began walking down the main road. I saw empty houses with broken doors, buried in weeds. What had that guy told me this weed was called? "La capitana, señor. A plague that waits for people to leave so it can overtake their homes. You'll see."

While passing a side street I saw a woman wrapped in her rebozo disappear as if she'd never existed. After that my feet resumed their march, and my eyes once again peered through gaping doorways. Until the woman with the rebozo once more crossed the street in front of me.

—Buenas noches! —she said.

I followed her with my eyes. Then shouted:

—Where does doña Eduviges live?

She pointed with her finger:

—Over there. The house by the bridge.

I noticed that her voice was made of human cords, that her mouth had teeth and a tongue that would engage and disengage as she spoke, and that her eyes were just like those of anyone else alive on earth.

It had grown dark.

She said "buenas noches" again. And although there were no children playing, nor doves, nor rooftops shaded blue, I felt that the town was alive. And that if all I heard was silence, it was because I hadn't yet grown accustomed to the silence. Maybe because my head was still full of sounds and voices.

Yes, filled with voices. And here, with the air so thin, they were easier to hear. They settled inside you, heavy. I remembered what my mother had told me: "*You'll hear me better there. I'll be closer to you. You'll find the voice of my memories closer to you there than that of my death, that is if death has ever had a voice.*" My mother . . . The living one.

I would've liked to tell her: "You were all wrong about this place. You led me astray. You sent me out to chase my own tail. To an abandoned town. Searching for someone who doesn't exist."

To find the house by the bridge, I followed the sound of the river. I knocked at the door, but to no avail. My hand swung in the air as if the wind had blown the door open. There was a woman standing there who said:

—Come in.

And I went in.

I STAYED IN COMALA. The muleteer continued on his way, although, before leaving, he said:

—I'm headed quite a bit farther, over there where you see the hills coming together. That's where I've got my house. You'd be more than welcome if you want to come along. But if you prefer to stay here, that's up to you. There's nothing wrong with looking around town, and you might even find someone still among the living.

I stayed. That was why I'd come.

—Where can I find a room? —I called after him, now almost shouting.

—Look for doña Eduviges, if she's still alive. Tell her I sent you.

—And what's your name?

—Abundio —he replied. But by then I couldn't make out his last name.

—I'M EDUVIGES DYADA. Come in.

It seemed as if she'd been waiting for me. Everything was ready, she explained, and she had me follow her through a long series of dark rooms that appeared empty. But that wasn't the case. As I grew accustomed to the darkness and to the thread of light that trailed behind us, I began to make out shadows on both sides, and I sensed we were walking through a narrow opening between countless bundles.

—What's all this? —I asked.

—Just things —she said—. The house is full of things. Everyone who moved away chose my house as the place to store

. . . .

their stuff, yet nobody's come back for it. But the room I've saved for you is way in the back. I keep it empty in case someone shows up. So, you're her son?

—Whose son? —I asked.

—Doloritas's.

—Yes, but how'd you know?

—She told me you'd be coming. Today, in fact. That you'd come today.

—Who? My mother?

—Yes, her.

I didn't know what to think. Nor did she offer any clues:

—This is your room —she said.

It didn't have any doors, other than the one we'd just come through. She lit a candle, and I saw that the room was empty.

—There's nothing to lie down on —I told her.

—Don't worry. You must be tired, and sleep is a good mattress for fatigue. Tomorrow morning I'll arrange a bed. As you know, it's not easy to have everything perfectly put together last minute. People need some warning, and your mother didn't say a thing until just now.

—My mother —I said—, my mother's dead.

—So that's why her voice sounded so weak, as if it had to travel quite a distance just to get here. Now I understand. How long's it been since she passed?

—Seven days now.

—Poor thing. She must've felt abandoned. We promised to die together. To leave this world at the same time, to give each other courage on that final journey, if any were needed, or if we were to have any problems. We were the best of friends. Didn't she ever mention me?

—No, never.

—That's strange. We were still young back then, of course. And she was just married. But we loved each other a lot. Your mother was so pretty, or rather so sweet, that it was a pleasure to love her. You couldn't help but love her. So, she beat me to it, huh? But you can be sure I'll catch up to her. No one knows better than I do just how far we are from Heaven, but I also know a shortcut. God willing, it's about dying at a time of your own choosing rather than according to His time. Or, you might say, it's about forcing His hand a bit early. Forgive me for speaking to you as family, it's because I consider you my son. Yes, I often said: "Dolores's boy should've been mine." Later I'll tell you why. For now, let's just say I'm going to catch up to your mother on one of the roads that lead to eternity.

I was sure then that the woman had gone mad. Later, I wasn't sure of anything. It felt as if I were in a strange land, and I just let myself be dragged along. My body seemed to be floating, and then it gave way, and with its moorings let loose, anyone could've played with it as if it were a bundle of rags.

—I'm tired —I said.

—First come have a bite to eat. A little something. Anything'll do.

—I'll come. I'll come later.

WATER DRIPPING FROM the roof tiles was making a hole in the sand of the patio. It sounded: drip, drip, and then again drip as it landed on a laurel leaf that bounced around while staying stuck in a crack between the bricks. The storm had moved on. An occasional breeze would shake the leaves of the pomegranate tree, making them shed a heavy rain whose shimmering drops left a pattern on the ground before turning to mist. The chickens, crouching tightly as if asleep, suddenly flapped their wings and headed out to the patio, where they pecked furiously to grab worms forced out of the ground by the rain. As the clouds moved on, the sun threw its light on the rocks making them shimmer with color; it drank the water from the earth and made the leaves shine as they played in the gentle wind.

—What's taking you so long in the privy, young man?

—Nothing, mamá.

—If you stay in there much longer, a snake will come out and bite you.

—Yes, mamá.

«I was thinking of you, Susana. Up in those green hills. When we'd fly kites during the windy season. As we played on top of that hill, we'd hear the sounds of life rising from the town below, and the string, pulled by the wind, would get away from us. "Help me, Susana." And soft hands would tighten around mine. "Let out more string."

»We'd laugh at the wind and find each other's eyes as the string slipped through our fingers and ran with the wind before breaking with a faint cracking sound as if it had been cut by the wings of a passing bird. Then way above us that paper bird would flail downward, dragging its loose tail behind until it became lost in the green earth below.

»Your lips were moist as if kissed by the dew.»

—I said to come out of the privy, young man.

—Yes, mamá. I'm coming.

«I was thinking of you. When you stood there looking at me with your aquamarine eyes.»

He looked up and saw his mother in the doorway.

—What's taking you so long to come out? What're you doing in there?

—I'm thinking.

—And you can't do that someplace else? It's unhealthy to spend so much time in the privy. Besides, you should be doing something productive. Why don't you go help your grandmother shell the corn?

—I'm going, mamá. I'm going.

—**GRANDMA, I'M HERE** to help shell the corn.

—We're done, but now we're gonna grind chocolate. Where'd you take off to? We looked for you all through the storm.

—I was in the other patio.

—And what were you doing? Praying?

—No, Grandma, I was just watching the rain.

His grandmother looked at him with those eyes of hers that were half gray and half yellow and that seemed to know what someone was hiding inside.

—Well now, go clean out the mill.

«You've hidden yourself away, Susana, hundreds of meters high, way above the clouds, farther away than all other things. Hidden in the immensity of God, behind His Divine Providence, in a place where I can't reach you, nor even see you, and where my words won't find you.»

—Grandma, the mill's not working, the grinder's broken.

—That Micaela must have been using it to grind corncobs. I can't get her to break that bad habit, but there's not a whole lot we can do about it now.

—Can't we buy another one? This one's so old it hasn't been working right anyway.

—You're right. Although after what we spent to bury your grandfather and the tithings we gave to the church, there's no money left. Even so, we'll sacrifice somewhere and buy another one. Why don't you go see doña Inés Villalpando and ask her if she can't give us one on credit through October. We'll pay her out of the harvest.

—Yes, Grandma.

—And while you're there, ask her to add a sifter and a pair of pruning shears to round out the order. With how fast these plants are growing they'll soon run us out of the place. I wouldn't have reason to complain if I were still in that big house, with its open spaces. But your grandfather ruined that when we moved here. It must be God's will: nothing turns out exactly as you want. Tell doña Inés we'll pay what we owe out of the harvest.

—Yes, Grandma.

There were hummingbirds. It was the season. You could hear their wings whirring among jasmine bushes that had bent over from the weight of their flowers.

He walked by the shelf displaying an image of the Sacred Heart, and there he found twenty-four centavos. He left the four centavos and took the twenty.

Before he could leave, his mother stopped him:

—Where are you headed?

—To see doña Inés Villalpando about a new mill. Ours is broken.

—Ask her for a meter of black taffeta, like this —and she gave him a sample—. Have her put it on our account.

—All right, mamá.

—On your way home buy me some cafiaspirina pills. You'll find some money in the flowerpot in the hallway.

He found a peso. He left the twenty centavos and grabbed the peso.

«Now I've got enough money for whatever I want,» he thought.

—Pedro! —they yelled after him—. Pedro!

But by then he couldn't hear a thing. He was already a long way off.

THAT NIGHT IT RAINED AGAIN. He listened to the bubbling water for a long while; at some point he must have fallen asleep, because when he awoke, the only thing he could hear was a faint drizzle. The windowpanes were dark, while on the outside, raindrops slid down in thick threads as if they were tears. "I watched the raindrops as they glistened in the lightning, and with every breath I took I let out a sigh, and every time I thought, it was of you, Susana."

The rain changed into a breeze. He heard: "Forgiveness of sins and resurrection of the flesh. Amen." It came from inside the house, where a few women were finishing the rosary. They got up, returned the birds to their cages, bolted the door, turned out the lights.

Only the light of the night remained, the hissing of the rain like the murmuring of crickets . . .

—Why didn't you go and pray the rosary? We're making a novena for your grandfather.

His mother stood in the doorway, a candle in her hand. Her long shadow stretched toward the ceiling, unfurled, while the rafters pushed it back, breaking it into fragments.

—I'm too sad —he said.

She turned away and blew out the candle. As she closed the door, she opened the faucet of her tears, and her wailing could be heard long after it merged with the sound of the rain.

The church clock rang out the hours, one after another, one after another, as if time had contracted.

—YES, IT'S TRUE, I was close to being your mother. She never told you?

—No. She only told me good things. I heard about you from the muleteer who brought me here, a man named Abundio.

—He's a good one, that Abundio. He still remembers me, then? I used to give him a little something for each traveler he'd send my way. It was a good deal for both of us. Unfortunately, the times have changed, and nobody keeps in touch with us now that things are so much worse around here. So, he told you to come see me?

—He told me to look for you.

—I can't thank him enough. He was a good man and very reliable. He's the one who took care of our mail, and he kept doing that even after he lost his hearing. I remember the awful day he suffered his accident. It bothered all of us because we liked him so much. We'd give him our letters, and he'd bring others back. He let us know how things were on the other side of the world, and I'm sure he'd tell them what was going on with us. He was quite the chatterbox. Later on, not so much, when he stopped talking. Said it made no sense to go on about things he couldn't hear and that had no sound to them, that gave off no flavor whatsoever. It all happened when one of those rockets we use to ward off waterspouts, those things everyone calls "culebras de agua," exploded right next to his head. After that, he stopped talking, even though he wasn't actually mute. In any event, he kept on being a good person.

—The one I'm talking about could hear just fine.

—Must not be him, then. Besides, Abundio died already. He must have died already. So you see? It couldn't have been him.

—That sounds right.

—Anyway, getting back to what I was saying about your mother . . .

As I listened to her, I began to pay closer attention to the woman standing before me. I imagined she must've endured quite a few hard years. Her face was transparent, as if without blood, and her hands were shriveled; shriveled and full of wrinkles. You couldn't see her eyes. She was wearing an ancient white dress that was covered in ruffles, and from her neck, fastened to a cord, hung an image of María Santísima del Refugio with the inscription: "Refuge of Sinners."

—. . . The guy I'm talking about worked at the Media Luna "taming horses." Said his name was Inocencio Osorio, although we all knew him by the awful name of El Saltaperico on account of him being so light on his feet and fond of hopping around. My compadre Pedro said he was a natural at breaking colts; but it's also true he plied another trade: that of "provocateur," arousing people's fantasies. That's what he really did. And he drew your mother in like he'd done with so many other women. Myself included. Once when I was feeling unwell, he showed up and said: "I'm here to work you over so you'll feel better." And what he meant by that was that he'd begin rubbing you down. He'd start with the tips of your fingers, then he'd massage your hands, followed by your arms, until finally and without warning he'd go after your legs, and soon he'd have you all heated up. And as he worked on you, he'd talk about your future. He'd fall into a trance and roll his eyes while chanting and cursing, spitting all over your body like the gypsies do. At times he'd end up buck naked, because that's what we wanted, or so he'd say. And every now and then he'd get something right; after all, when you shoot in that many directions, sooner or later you're gonna hit something.

»As it turns out, when she went to see him, this Osorio guy gazed into your mother's future and told her she "should avoid lying with a man that night, since the moon was fraught with danger."

»Dolores came to me all worked up saying she couldn't do it, that there was no way she was gonna sleep with Pedro Páramo that evening. It was her wedding night. And there I was trying to convince her she couldn't trust Osorio, that he was little more than a two-faced con artist.

»—I can't —she told me—. Go in my place. He won't notice.

»Needless to say, I was quite a bit younger than she was. And not as brown, but that's not something you notice in the dark.

»—It's not gonna work, Dolores, you've got to go yourself.

»—Do me this one favor. I'll pay you back with others.

»In those days, your mother had gentle eyes. If anything about her was pretty, it was those eyes. They knew how to persuade.

»—Go in my place —she begged.

»So I went.

»I relied on the darkness and on something your mother knew nothing about: I had a thing for Pedro Páramo as well.

»I got into bed with him, happily, filled with desire. I cuddled up next to his body; but the day's excitement had left him worn out, and he spent the night snoring. The only thing he did was to intertwine his legs with mine.

»Before the sun came out, I got up and went to see Dolores. I told her:

»—Go now. It's a new day.

»—What did he do to you? —she asked.

»—I'm still not sure —I responded.

»You were born the following year. But not to me, although you sure came close to being mine.

»Maybe your mother was too ashamed to tell you any of this.

". . . *Green fields. Seeing the horizon rise and fall as the wheat sways in the wind, the afternoon rippling as it is battered by the rain. The color of the earth, the scent of alfalfa and bread. A town that smells of spilled honey . . .*"

»She always loathed Pedro Páramo. "Doloritas! Did you tell them to get my breakfast ready?" Your mother would get up before dawn. She'd light the nixtenco stove. The cats would rouse with the smell of burning wood. She'd scamper here and there, lorded over by that clowder of cats. "Doña Doloritas!"

»How many times must your mother have heard him call her name? "Doña Doloritas, this food is cold. This won't do." How many times? And even though she was no stranger to hardship, those gentle eyes of hers finally went numb.

". . . *And everything tastes like orange blossoms wrapped in the warmth of the season.*"

»That's when she began to sigh.

»—Why are you always sighing, Doloritas?

»I had gone with them that afternoon. We were out in the fields watching flocks of thrushes pass overhead. A lone vulture hovered in the sky.

»—Why are you sighing, Doloritas?

»—I wish I were a vulture so I could fly to where my sister lives.

»—That's all I needed to hear, doña Doloritas. You'll leave immediately to go see your sister. Let's head back. Get your bags packed. That's all I needed to hear.

»And your mother headed out:

»—So long, don Pedro.

»—Adiós, Doloritas!

»She left the Media Luna for good. Some months later, I asked Pedro Páramo how she was doing.

»—She loved her sister more than she did me. I'm sure she's happy there. Besides, she was getting under my skin. I have no plans to ask about her, if that's what you're getting at.

»—But how will they survive?

»—Let God take care of them.

". . . *Make him pay dearly, my son, for having abandoned us.*"

»And that was the last we heard from her until now when she let me know you'd be coming to see me.»

—A lot happened after that —I said—. We were living with my Aunt Gertrudis in Colima, but she felt we were a burden and rubbed it in our faces. "Why don't you go back to your husband?" she'd always ask my mother.

»—Has he sent for me, by chance? I'm not going back unless he sends for me. I came because I wanted to see you. Because I loved you, that's why.

»—I understand. But it's time for you to leave.

»—As if that were up to me.»

. . . .

I thought that woman was listening to me; but I noticed her head was cocked as if she were hearing some distant sound. Then she said:

—When will you rest?

«THE DAY YOU LEFT I knew I'd never see you again. As you walked away, the afternoon sun bathed you in a reddish hue, in the blood red sky of dusk. You were smiling. You were escaping a town about which you'd often said: "I love this place because of you, but I hate it because of everything else, even for having been born here." I thought: "She's not coming back, she'll never come back."»

—Why are you here at this hour? Aren't you working?

—No, Grandma. Rogelio wanted me to look after his little boy. I'm walking him around. It's too much to look after both things: the kid and the telegraph, especially when Rogelio spends his days drinking beer down at the pool hall. Not to mention he doesn't pay me anything.

—You're not there to earn money, but to learn. You can't start making demands until you have a bit of experience. Maybe someday they'll even put you in charge. Until then, have a bit of patience and, more importantly, a bit of humility. If they ask you to take the boy out for a walk, then do it, for God's sake. You have to do what you're told.

—Let others do what they're told, Grandma, I'm not one for following orders.

—You're a peculiar young man! I've got a feeling things aren't going to turn out well for you, Pedro Páramo.

—**WHAT IS IT**, doña Eduviges?

She shook her head as if she were waking from a dream.

—It's Miguel Páramo's horse, galloping along the road to the Media Luna.

—So someone still lives out at the Media Luna?

—No, no one lives there.

—Then . . . ?

—It's just his horse, always out and about. The two were inseparable. It wanders all over the place looking for him and always comes back at this hour. Seems the poor thing can't handle its own grief. Maybe even animals can feel when they've done something wrong, right?

—I don't understand. I haven't heard any sound coming from any horse.

—No?

—No.

—Then it must be my sixth sense. A gift from God, or perhaps a curse. You can't imagine how I've suffered because of it.

She was silent for a while and then added:

—It all began with Miguel Páramo. I'm the only one who knew what happened the night he died. I was already in bed when I heard his horse headed for the Media Luna. I thought it strange since he never returned at that time. He always came home in the early hours of the morning. He'd set out for this town called Contla to visit a girlfriend of his, quite a ways off. He'd leave early and it'd take him a while to get back. But that night he never returned . . . Do you hear it now? Surely you can hear it. It's coming home.

—I don't hear a thing.

—Then it's just me. Anyway, getting back to my story, what I said about Miguel not making it home is not completely true. His horse was still passing by when I sensed that someone was knocking at the window. You'll have to decide if it was just my imagination. What I know for sure is that something was pushing me to see who it was. And it was him, it was Miguel Páramo.

I wasn't surprised since there was a time he'd spend his nights sleeping at my house, in bed with me. At least until he found this other girl who got him all worked up.

»—What happened? —I asked Miguel Páramo—. Did she break it off?

»—No. She still loves me —he said—. It's just that I couldn't get to her. The town was nowhere to be found. There was a lot of fog or smoke or who knows what. What I do know is that Contla doesn't exist. I went way past where it should've been, by my calculations, and I didn't see a thing. I'm here to let you know what happened because you understand me. If I told anyone else in Comala they'd say I was crazy, like they always do.

»—No. Not crazy, Miguel. You must be dead. Remember how everyone said that horse was going to kill you some day. Remember that, Miguel Páramo. Maybe you were doing something foolish, but that's beside the point.

»—The only thing I did was go over that stone fence my father recently ordered put up. I had El Colorado jump it so we could get back on the path without going so far around like you have to do now. I'm sure I made the jump and kept on going, but, as I already said, there was nothing but smoke, smoke, and more smoke.

»—Tomorrow your father's gonna be devastated —I told him—. I feel for him. Now go rest in peace, Miguel. I'm grateful you came to say goodbye.

»And I closed the window.

»Before dawn a worker from the Media Luna showed up to say:

»—The patrón, don Pedro, is asking for you. Young Miguel has passed away. He wants you to keep him company.

»—I'm already aware —I told him—. Did they ask you to cry?

»—Yes, don Fulgor told me to cry while giving you the news.

»—Okay then. Tell don Pedro I'll be there. How long's it been since they brought him in?

»—Not quite a half hour. If it'd been sooner, maybe they could've saved him. Although the doctor who examined him says he'd been cold quite a while. We knew something was up when El Colorado came home alone and made such a fuss no one could sleep. You know how much he and that horse loved each other, so much that I almost think the animal is suffering more than don Pedro. It won't eat nor sleep and just runs around. As if it knew, you know? As if it felt broken and torn up on the inside.

»—Don't forget to close the door on the way out.

»And the worker from the Media Luna took off.

»You ever hear a dead man moaning?» she asked me.

—No, doña Eduviges.

—All the better.

DROPS FALL, ONE AFTER ANOTHER, through the stone filter. As fresh water emerges from the rock one hears the sound it makes as it drips into a clay pitcher. One listens. Hearing whispers. Hearing feet that scrape against the floor, that walk back and forth. The dripping continues nonstop. The pitcher overflows, sending water across the wet ground.

«Wake up!» someone calls.

He recognizes the sound of the voice. He tries to imagine who it belongs to, but his body goes limp, and he drifts back to sleep, crushed by the weight of his slumber. Hands tug at the blankets and draw them close while beneath their warmth a body hides from the world in search of peace.

«Wake up!» someone says again.

The voice shakes him by the shoulders, forcing him to straighten his body. He half opens his eyes. Again, there's the sound of water as it drips from the stone filter into the clay pitcher. And the sound of footsteps shuffling . . . And of weeping.

He heard the weeping. That's what woke him for good: a calm and thin lament, that perhaps on account of its being so thin was able to seep through the confusion of his dreams and reach the very spot where dread had made a home.

He slowly got up and saw the face of a woman leaning against the door frame, a face still obscured by the night, weeping.

—Why are you crying, mamá? —he asked, since he recognized his mother's features as soon as his feet hit the ground.

—Your father's dead —she told him.

And then, as if the coils of her sorrow had snapped loose, she reeled, once, and then again, and then again, until someone's hands grabbed her shoulders and put an end to her trembling.

The morning sky was beginning to show through the doorway. There were no stars. Just a leaden sky, gray, not yet illuminated by the brightness of the sun. A dull light, as if the day were not about to commence, but rather as if night were beginning to fall.

Outside in the patio, footsteps, as if people were walking in circles. Muffled noises. And here inside, that woman standing in the doorway, her body holding back the day's arrival, allowing only fragments of the sky to pass through her arms, and below her a shattering of light, a drizzle of light as if the floor beneath her feet were inundated with tears. And then the sobbing. Once again that gentle but penetrating weeping, and a grief causing her body to shudder.

—They've killed your father.

—And you, Mother? Who killed you?

«THERE'S WIND, AND SUN, and clouds. Above us a blue sky and beyond that perhaps there's singing, maybe in voices sweeter than our own . . . In a word, there's hope. There's hope for us, a hope set against our suffering.

»But not for you, Miguel Páramo, who died without forgiveness and will never receive God's grace.«

Father Rentería walked around the body and said mass, brushing the words aside. He rushed to get it over with and left without giving the final blessing to those who had filled the church.

—Father, we want you to bless him!

—No! —he said, shaking his head—. I won't do it. He was an evil man, and he won't enter the Kingdom of Heaven. God would be offended if I interceded on his behalf.

As he spoke, he struggled to steady his hands and conceal his trembling. To no avail.

The corpse weighed heavy on everyone's soul. It was laid out on a dais in the middle of the church, surrounded by fresh candles, by flowers, and by a father who stood behind it, alone, waiting for the wake to end.

Father Rentería walked by Pedro Páramo trying not to brush against his shoulders. He gently raised and lowered the aspergillum to sprinkle the body with holy water, while a murmur that might have been a prayer emerged from his mouth. Then he knelt, and everyone knelt with him:

—Have mercy on Thy servant, O Lord.

—May he rest in peace, amen —the voices answered.

And just as bitterness again began to fill his soul, he noticed that everyone was leaving the church, taking the body of Miguel Páramo with them.

Pedro Páramo approached and knelt by his side:

—I know you hated him, Father. And with good reason. Some say my son's the one who killed your brother. And there's that thing with your niece, Ana, who you say he raped. Not to mention the constant derision and disrespect you had to endure from him. Anyone would understand such reasons. But forget all that now, Father. Think of him and forgive him, as perhaps God has forgiven him.

He placed a handful of gold coins on the prayer bench and got up:

—Accept this as an offering for your church.

By then, the building was empty. Two men waited in the doorway for Pedro Páramo. He joined them, and together they followed behind the coffin that had paused for them to catch up, resting on the shoulders of four overseers from the Media Luna.

Father Rentería collected the coins one by one and approached the altar.

—These belong to Thee —he said—. He can buy salvation. Thou wilt know if this is the price. As for me, Lord, I place myself at Thy feet and ask only for that which is just or unjust, as we all are given to ask for . . . For my part, Lord, condemn him.

He closed the chapel.

He walked into the sacristy and threw himself into one of the corners, where he wept out of shame and sorrow until he had no more tears to shed.

—All right, Lord, Thy will be done —he said.

AT SUPPER, HE DRANK his chocolate, just as he did every night. He felt at ease.

—Hey, Anita. You know who they buried today?

—No, Uncle.

—You remember Miguel Páramo?

—Yes, Uncle.

—Well, it was him.

Ana lowered her head.

—You're sure it was him, really?

—Completely sure, no, Uncle. I never saw his face. It was night when he took me, and it was dark.

—So, how'd you know it was Miguel Páramo?

—Because he said so: "It's me, Miguel Páramo, Ana. Don't be afraid." That's what he said.

—But you knew he was responsible for the death of your father, didn't you?

—Yes, Uncle.

—So, what did you do to push him away?

—I didn't do anything.

For a while they fell silent. The warm breeze could be heard passing through the arrayán leaves.

—He said that's why he had come: to apologize and to ask me to forgive him. Without getting out of bed, I let him know: "The window's open." And he came in. First thing he did was grab me in his arms, as if that were the best way to express regret for what he'd done. And I smiled at him. I thought about what you'd taught me: that we should never hate anyone. I smiled to let him know this, but then I thought he probably couldn't see my face, since I couldn't see him either, on account of how dark the night was. I just felt him on top of me as he began doing bad things to me.

»I was sure he was gonna kill me. That's what I thought, Uncle. I even stopped thinking so maybe I'd already be dead before he took my life. But he must not have had the courage to go through with it.

»I knew he hadn't when I opened my eyes and saw the morning light coming through the open window. Before that moment, it felt as if I no longer existed.»

—But there must be something you can be sure of. His voice. Didn't you recognize his voice?

—I didn't recognize him at all. All I knew was that he'd killed my father. I'd never seen him before, and after that I never saw him again. I couldn't have, Uncle.

—But you knew who he was.

—Yes. And what he was. And I know by now he's got to be in the very depths of Hell, because that's what I've asked all the saints for with all my heart.

—You mustn't be too sure of that, my child. You never know how many others are praying on his behalf at this very moment. You're just one person. A single petition against thousands of others. And among those are some that are even more ardent than your own, like the one from his father.

He was about to say: "Besides, I've already given him absolution." But it was only a thought. He had no desire to cause more pain to that poor girl and her half-broken soul. Instead, he took her by the arm and said:

—Let's give thanks to the Lord our God, for He has taken him from this earth where he caused so much harm, even if now He has received him in Heaven.

A HORSE GALLOPED BY, over where the main road intersects with the road to Contla. No one saw it. Nonetheless, a woman who had been waiting just outside of town mentioned that she had seen the horse running hard, its legs doubled over as if it were about to fall forward onto its head. She recognized it as Miguel Páramo's sorrel. She even thought: "That animal's gonna kill itself." She was still watching when the horse, without breaking its stride, straightened up and turned its head to look back as if frightened by something it had left behind.

These stories made their way to the Media Luna the night of the burial, as the men were resting from their long hike out to the cemetery.

As people do everywhere, they chatted before heading to bed.

—This was a painful death to bear —said Terencio Lubianes—. My shoulders are still sore.

—Mine too —said his brother Ubillado—. Even my bunions got worse. All because the patrón wanted us in shoes. It wasn't even a feast day, am I right, Toribio?

—What do you want me to say? I think it was about time he died.

Pretty soon more gossip arrived from Contla, traveling on the latest oxcart.

—They say his soul is wandering out and about. People have seen it knocking at some girl's window. Looked just like him. In leather chaps and all.

—You really think don Pedro, with that temper of his, would let his son keep chasing women? Just imagine what he'd do if he were to find out: "—Look here —he'd say—. You're dead now. Stay down there in your grave and keep quiet. Leave this business to us." And if he were to see him strolling around, I bet he'd put him back in the ground for good.

—You're right about that, Isaías. That old man doesn't put up with nonsense.

The oxcart driver continued on his way: "I'm just telling you what I heard."

There were falling stars, dropping as if the heavens were drizzling fire.

—Just look —said Terencio— at the commotion they've got going on up there.

—Must be celebrating Miguelito's arrival —added Jesús.

—Isn't that supposed to be a bad omen?

—Bad for who?

—Maybe your sister's feeling lonely and wants him back.

—Who are you talking to?

—To you.

—We'd better get going, fellas. We've been on the road a long time and we've got to get up early tomorrow.

And they dissolved like shadows.

THERE WERE FALLING STARS. The lights of Comala went out.

That's when the sky took control of the night.

Father Rentería tossed in his bed, unable to sleep:

«All this is my fault —he told himself—. All because I'm afraid of offending those who provide for me. And that's the truth: they're the ones who give me what I need to survive. I get nothing from the poor, and prayers won't fill my stomach. That's how it's been so far. And these are the consequences. It's all my fault. I've betrayed those who love me and those who put their faith in me, asking me to intercede before God on their behalf. But what have they gained for that faith? Entrance into Heaven? Or the cleansing of their souls? And what good is it for them to purify their souls if at the last moment . . . I can still see María Dyada's face when she came begging me to save her sister Eduviges:

»—She was always serving others. She gave them everything she had. She even provided them, all of them, with sons. She'd show those children around for someone to recognize them as their own. But no one ever did. Then she'd say: "In that case, I'll be their father as well, even though it's only by chance that I became their mother." They took advantage of her hospitality by appealing to a kind disposition that never wanted to offend or cause a rift with others.

»—But she killed herself. She acted in defiance of God.

»—She had no other choice. Even that decision was made from the goodness of her heart.

»—She came up short at the last hour —that's what I told her—. At the last hour. So many good deeds accumulated toward salvation, only to lose them in an instant!

»—But she didn't lose them. She died full of sorrow. And sorrow . . . You once told us something about sorrow that I no longer remember. It was that type of sorrow that took her life. She died all twisted up, choking on her own blood. I can still see the expression on her face, one of the most miserable faces a human being has ever made.

»—Perhaps through a lot of prayer.

»—Let's say a lot of prayers, Father.

»—I mean perhaps, just maybe, by saying a few Gregorian masses. But for that we'd need to ask for assistance, send for priests. And that costs money.

»And right there in front of my eyes was that gaze of María Dyada, a poor woman bursting with children.

»—I don't have any money. You already know that, Father.

»—Let's leave things as they are. Let's put our faith in God.

»—Yes, Father.»

Why did her gaze seem to gain courage in this moment of resignation? What would it cost him to grant forgiveness, when it is so easy to say a word or two, or even a hundred if that were needed to save a soul? What did he know of Heaven and Hell? Even so, hidden away in this town of little consequence, he knew quite well who the people were who deserved God's Glory. There was a list. He began reviewing the saints of the Catholic pantheon, beginning with those for that day: "Saint Nunilona, virgin and martyr; Anercio, bishop; Saints Salomé, widow, Alodia or Elodio and Nulina, virgins; Córdula and Donato." And he kept going. He was already feeling drowsy when he sat up in bed: "I'm going through a list of saints as if I were counting sheep."

He went outside and looked toward the heavens. It was raining stars. It was a sight he was sad to see since he would've preferred a calm sky. He heard roosters crowing. He felt the weight of the night as it covered the earth. The earth, "this vale of tears."

—ALL THE BETTER, Son. All the better —said Eduviges Dyada.

It was already late at night. The lamp burning in one of the corners of the room began to weaken, then it flickered and went out.

I sensed that the woman was getting up, and I imagined she'd go get a new lamp. I heard her footsteps as they moved farther and farther away. I stayed and waited.

After a while I realized she wasn't coming back, and I stood up as well. I advanced slowly, feeling my way in the dark, until I got to my room. I sat on the ground and waited for sleep to come.

I slept on and off, uneasily.

It was during a restless moment that I heard the scream. It was a long and dispirited howl like one you might hear from a drunkard: "A-y-y-y life, you don't deserve me!"

I sat straight up since what I heard seemed to emanate from right next to my ears. It might've come from the street, but I heard it inside, spread along the walls of my room. As I gained my bearings, everything was completely quiet, the only sound a moth falling through the air and the whispering of silence.

No, there was simply no way to fathom the depth of the silence that followed in the wake of that scream. As if all the air had drained from the earth. Not a sound. Not of breathing, not of a beating heart, as if the very din of existence had ceased. And just as that moment was beginning to pass and my nerves had started to settle, the scream came back and persisted for a long while: "At least grant me the right of those sent to the gallows to kick at the air!"

That's when the door flew open.

—Is that you, doña Eduviges? —I asked—. What's going on? Were you afraid?

—My name's not Eduviges. It's Damiana. I heard you were here and came to find you. I wanted to invite you to spend the night at my house. You'll be able to get some rest there.

—Damiana Cisneros? Aren't you one of the women who lived out at the Media Luna?

—That's where I live. That's why it's taken me a while to get here.

—My mother told me about a Damiana who took care of me after I was born. Would that be you . . . ?

—Yes, that's me. I've known you since you first opened your eyes.

—I'll come with you. I can't get any rest here with all the screaming. Didn't you hear all the racket? As if someone were being killed. Didn't you hear that just now?

—Perhaps it's an echo trapped inside here. It was in this very room where they hanged Toribio Aldrete quite a few years ago. They sealed the door afterward and left his body to dry out so he wouldn't find any peace. I can't imagine how you got in since there's no key to open the door.

—It was doña Eduviges who let me in. She said it was the only room available.

—Eduviges Dyada?

—That's her.

—Poor Eduviges. Her soul must still be in torment.

«I, FULGOR SEDANO, fifty-four years of age, single, administrator by occupation, qualified to initiate and pursue civil disputes, through legal authority and on my own behalf, do claim and allege the following . . .»

That's what he had said when he presented his complaint against Toribio Aldrete. And he ended with: "That my accusation is one of usufruct."

—No one's gonna say you don't have guts, don Fulgor. You're tough as nails, and not on account of the authority that props you up, but all on your own.

He remembered. That was the first thing Aldrete told him when they began drinking, supposedly as a way of celebrating the complaint:

—You and I are gonna use that paper to wipe ourselves, don Fulgor, since that's what it's good for. And you know it. Anyway, you did your part and followed orders; and you've let me know I can breathe easy after you had me quite worried, as you might expect. But now that I realize what this is all about, I just have to laugh. "Usufruct," you say. Your patrón should be ashamed of himself for something so ignorant.

He remembered. They were in Eduviges's guest house. He had even asked her:

—Say, Viges, can I use the back room?

—Any room you need, don Fulgor. Take them all if you'd like. Are your men going to stay the night?

—No, just one of them. Don't worry about us and head off to bed. Just leave us the key.

—So, as I was saying, don Fulgor —Toribio Aldrete remarked—. No one's gonna say you don't have guts, but I'm tired as hell of that son-of-a-bitch patrón of yours.

He remembered. That was the last coherent thing he heard him say. After that, he acted like a coward, crying like a baby. "The authority that props me up, is that what you said? The hell with you!"

HE KNOCKED AT THE DOOR of Pedro Páramo's house using the handle of his whip. He thought about the first time he'd done that, two weeks earlier. Just as he had done then, he waited a good while for anyone to answer. And this time, again, he examined the black bow hanging from the lintel above the door. Yet this time he refrained from commenting to himself: "What the hell! They've put one right on top of the other. The older one's faded, while the more recent one glistens as if it were made of silk, even though it's nothing more than a rag that's been dyed black."

The first time he came, he had waited so long he began to wonder if the house were empty. But just as he was leaving, the figure of Pedro Páramo had appeared.

—Come in, Fulgor.

This was only the second time they had ever met. The first moment he was the only one who took notice since back then Pedrito was still a newborn. And now this time. You might even count this as their first meeting. And Fulgor imagined he was speaking as an equal. Go figure! He took long steps to keep up, slapping his whip against his legs all the while: "He'll know soon enough I'm the one with all the answers. He'll figure it out. And why I'm here."

—Have a seat, Fulgor. We can talk at ease here.

They were in the corral. Pedro Páramo settled comfortably on a feed trough and waited.

—Why don't you have a seat?

—I'd prefer to stand, Pedro.

—Whatever you prefer. But don't forget the "don."

Who was that kid to talk to him like that? Not even his father, don Lucas Páramo, would have dared do that. Now suddenly this youngster, who had never set foot out at the Media Luna and who knew nothing about how the ranch was run was talking to him as if he were a farmhand. What the hell!

—How do things stand?

He felt that this was his chance. "It's my turn now," he thought.

—Not well. There's nothing left. We've sold the last of the livestock.

He began taking out the papers to show him just how bad the accounts were. And he was about to say: "We owe too much," when he heard:

—Who are we indebted to? I don't care how much we owe, just to who.

He read off a list of names. And ended by saying:

—There's nothing left to pay it all off. That's how things stand.

—And why's that?

—Because that family of yours used it all up. They took and took, without ever giving anything back. That all adds up. I said it all along: "They're gonna bleed this place dry." Well, that's what's happened. Although I do know of someone who'd be interested in buying the land. And they'd pay well. It'd be enough to cover the outstanding debts, and you'd have a bit left over. Just not a lot, I'm afraid.

—Would that someone be you?

—How could you believe it'd be me!

—I'd believe anything. Tomorrow we're gonna start putting our affairs in order. Beginning with the Preciado women. You said we owe them the most, right?

—Yes. And they're the ones we've paid the least. That father of yours always put them at the end of the line. I understand one of the sisters, Matilde, went to live in the city. I'm not sure if it was Guadalajara or Colima. And Lola, I mean, doña Dolores, was left in charge of everything. The Enmedio Ranch, that is. And she's the one we'll have to settle with.

—Tomorrow you'll ask Lola for her hand in marriage.

—But what makes you think she'd want me? I'm just an old man.

—You're gonna ask on my behalf. It has a certain charm, doesn't it? You'll tell her I'm very much in love with her. See if she's willing. While you're at it, ask Father Rentería to make the arrangements. How much money do you have?

—None, don Pedro.

—Well, promise him something. Tell him we'll pay him when we can. I'm pretty sure he won't cause problems. Get it done first thing tomorrow.

—And what about that thing with Aldrete?

—What about Aldrete? You mentioned the Preciado women, the Fregosos, and the Guzmáns. Why's Aldrete coming up now?

—It concerns property lines. He's had his men put up fencing, and now he wants us to finish what's left, to clearly divide our lands.

—Leave that for later. You don't need to worry about fencing. There aren't gonna be any fences. The land doesn't have boundaries. Think about this, Fulgor, but don't say anything to anyone. For now, just make arrangements with Lola. Don't you want to sit down?

—I'll have a seat, don Pedro. Truth be told, I'm beginning to like working with you.

—Tell Lola whatever you need to, but let her know I love her. That's important. No question about it, Sedano, I love her. Because of her eyes, you know? Get it done first thing in the morning. I'll take care of your duties as administrator. Don't worry about the Media Luna.

«WHERE THE HELL would that kid have learned those tricks? —Fulgor Sedano thought as he headed back out to the Media Luna—. I didn't expect anything from him. "He's useless," my

patrón, the late don Lucas, used to say. "A good-for-nothing." I
agreed with him. "When I die, you're gonna want to look for different work, Fulgor." "Of course, don Lucas." "I tell you, Fulgor,
I even tried sending him to the seminary to see if that might give
him a way of feeding himself and taking care of his mother when
I'm gone. But he won't even make up his mind to do that." "You
don't deserve that, don Lucas." "Don't count on him for anything,
not even to take care of me in my old age. He's turned out bad,
Fulgor, what else can I say?" "It's a real shame, don Lucas."»

And now this. If he weren't so fond of the Media Luna, there's
no way he would've come to see him. He would've taken off
without saying a word. But he cared too much for this land.
The bare, rolling hills that had been worked so hard, yet kept
accepting the plow, giving more and more of themselves . . .
The Media Luna that he loved so much . . . With more lands to
come: "I'm talking to you, Enmedio Ranch, come on over." He
could see that property added on, as if it already belonged. What
does one woman matter anyway? "Damn right!" he said. And he
slapped the whip against his legs as he passed through the main
door of the hacienda.

IT WAS EASY TO GET Dolores on board. Her eyes even spar-
kled, and her eagerness showed on her face.

—Forgive me for blushing, don Fulgor. I had no idea don
Pedro had ever noticed me.

—He can't sleep, thinking of you.

—But he could choose anyone. There are so many pretty
girls in Comala. What'll they say when they find out?

—He only thinks about you, Dolores. Nobody else.

—You're making me shiver, don Fulgor. I never imagined.

—It's because he's so reserved. Don Lucas Páramo, may he
rest in peace, told him you weren't worthy of him. And he kept

quiet out of pure obedience. Now that his father's gone, there's nothing to stand in the way. It was the first decision he made, although it's taken me a while to follow through, on account of how busy I've been. Let's set the wedding for the day after tomorrow. How does that sound to you?

—Isn't that rather soon? I don't have anything prepared. I'll need to arrange for a trousseau. And write a letter to my sister. No, I'd better send a messenger. Even so, I won't be ready before the eighth of April. Today's the first. Yes, I couldn't be ready until the eighth. Ask him to wait just a few short days.

—He'd prefer to do it right now. If you're worried about the trousseau, we can take care of that. Don Pedro's deceased mother would want you to wear her dress. It's a family tradition.

—But there's something else about that date. Women's issues, if you know what I mean. Goodness! I'm mortified to say it out loud, don Fulgor. You're making me blush. It's my lunar cycle. Oh dear! I'm so embarrassed.

—And so what? Marriage isn't about whether it's your time of the month or not. It's about loving each other. And when you've got that, nothing else matters.

—But I don't think you're understanding me, don Fulgor.

—I understand perfectly. The wedding's set for the day after tomorrow.

As he left, her arms were still outstretched, pleading for one week, just one more week.

«I can't forget to tell don Pedro —damn, that young Pedro sure is cunning!— to let the judge know the property will be owned jointly. "Don't forget, Fulgor, to tell him that first thing tomorrow."»

Dolores, on the other hand, ran to the kitchen with a pitcher to begin boiling some water: "Let's see if I can get this started as quickly as possible. Maybe as early as tonight. Even so, it's gonna last my usual three days. Nothing I can do about it. I'm so happy!"

Just so happy! Thank you, God, for giving me don Pedro." Then
she added: "Even if later he despises me."

—**SHE'S BEEN ASKED**, and she's more than willing. The priest
wants sixty pesos to overlook the marriage banns. I told him he'd
be paid in due time. Says he needs to fix the altar and that his
dining table is falling apart. I promised we'd send a new one. He
says you never attend mass. I promised him you would. He also
says you haven't paid any tithes since your grandmother passed.
I told him not to worry. He's fine with that.

—Didn't you ask Dolores for an advance?

—No, patrón. Truth is, I didn't dare. She was so happy, and
I didn't want to spoil her enthusiasm.

—You're such a child.

«Good Lord! Me a child. With fifty-five years under my belt?
He's just getting started in life, and I'm a few steps from the
grave.»

—I didn't want to dampen her spirits.

—Even so, you're still a child.

—Whatever you say, patrón.

—Next week, you're going to pay a visit to Aldrete. And
you'll tell him to redo the fencing. He's trespassing on land that
belongs to the Media Luna.

—His measurements are accurate. I'm sure of it.

—Well, tell him he made a mistake. That he's figured wrong.
Tear down the fencing if that's what it takes.

—And what about the laws?

—What laws, Fulgor? From now on, we'll be the ones making the laws. You have any troublemakers working at the Media
Luna?

—Sure, there's one or two.

—Send them on a job to visit Aldrete. Then you file a complaint accusing him of "usufruct," or whatever else you come up with. Remind him that Lucas Páramo is dead. That he's gonna need to make new arrangements with me.

The sky was still blue, with only a few clouds. High above, there were gusts of wind, while down below it was just heating up.

HE KNOCKED AGAIN with the handle of his whip, just to make a point, since he knew no one was going to open up until Pedro Páramo was good and ready. As he examined the lintel above the doorway, he said: "Those black ribbons sure are nice, one for every person who's gone."

Just then the door opened, and he went in.

—Come in, Fulgor. Is the thing with Toribio Aldrete taken care of?

—Everything's settled, patrón.

—That leaves our business with the Fregosos. Let's save that for later. Right now, I'm busy with my "honeymoon."

—THIS TOWN IS FULL of echoes. It's as if they were trapped in the gaps of the walls or beneath the cobblestones. As you walk, you feel someone following in your footsteps. You hear things rustling. Laughter. Old laughter, as if it were tired of laughing. And voices that are weary from overuse. You hear all those things. I imagine the day will come when these sounds wither away.

That's what Damiana Cisneros told me as we walked across town.

—There was a time when I could hear the commotion of a party that kept going night after night for quite some time. The

noise made it all the way out to the Media Luna. Until finally
I came down to see what the fuss was about, and this is what
I found: just what we're seeing right now. Nothing. Not a soul.
The streets every bit as empty as they are now.

»Later, I stopped hearing those noises. It's exhausting being
happy. That's why I wasn't at all surprised when it came to an
end.

»That's right —Damiana Cisneros repeated—. This town
is full of echoes. They don't scare me anymore. I hear the dogs
howling, and I just let them howl. And on blustery days you see
the wind as it blows the leaves here and there, even when it's easy
to see there aren't any trees around these parts. There must've
been at some point. Otherwise, where would all the leaves have
come from?

»The worst thing is when you hear people talking, and their
voices sound as if they were coming from a fissure yet are so clear
you might recognize them. It just so happens that as I was on
my way here, I came across a wake and paused to say the Lord's
Prayer. I was still praying when a woman broke from the group
and came over to say:

»—Damiana! Pray to God for me, Damiana?

»She removed her rebozo and I recognized the face of my
sister Sixtina.

»—What're you doing here? —I asked.

»She then hurried back to hide among the other women.

»My sister Sixtina, if you didn't know, died when I was
twelve. She was the oldest. There were sixteen of us in the family,
so just imagine how long she's been gone. And look at her now,
still wandering the earth. So don't be frightened, Juan Preciado,
if you hear echoes that are more recent.»

—Did my mother warn you I'd be coming as well? —I asked.

—No. By the way, whatever happened to your mother?

—She died —I said.

—She died, huh? What of?

—I never really knew. Perhaps it was sorrow. She used to sigh a lot.

—That's not good. Each sigh is like a sip of life that slowly gets away from us. She's dead, then?

—Yes. I thought you would've known.

—How would I have known? It's been years since I've known anything.

—Then how'd you find me?

—. . .

—Are you alive, Damiana? Tell me, Damiana!

Suddenly, I found myself alone in those empty streets. The windows of the houses open to the heavens, twisted weeds poking out. The walls peeling back to reveal moldering adobe bricks.

—Damiana! —I yelled—. Damiana Cisneros!

The echo responded: ". . . ana . . . neros! . . . ana . . . neros!"

I HEARD THE DOGS BARKING, as if I'd woken them.

I saw a man cross the street:

—Hey, you! —I called out.

—Hey, you! —my own voice replied.

And as if they were just around the corner, I heard women chatting:

—Look who's coming this way. Isn't that Filoteo Aréchiga?

—That's him. Pretend not to notice.

—Better yet, let's go. If he follows, it must mean he's interested in one of us. Who do you think he's after?

—It's got to be you.

—I'd say it's you.

—Quit rushing already. He stopped back at that corner.

—Looks like he didn't want either one of us, I guess?

—But what if he'd been after you or me? What then?

—Don't flatter yourself.

—It's better this way. All the gossips say he's the one who finds girls for don Pedro. We could've been in real trouble.

—Is that so? I don't want anything to do with that old man.

—We ought to be going.

—You're right. Let's get out of here.

NIGHT. QUITE A BIT past midnight. Voices:

—. . . I'm telling you, if the corn does well this year, I'll be able to pay you what I owe. But if I lose the crop, you'll simply have to wait.

—I'm not pushing. You know I've been more than fair with you. But that land's not yours. You're working fields that belong to someone else. Where you gonna get the money to pay me?

—Who says the land isn't mine?

—I heard you sold it to Pedro Páramo.

—I've never had anything to do with that man. That land's still mine.

—According to you, yes, but everyone else says it belongs to him.

—Have them say it to my face.

—Let's be frank, Galileo. I like you a lot, and you're my sister's husband. No one doubts you treat her well. But you can't say you didn't sell your land.

—I'm telling you I didn't sell to anyone.

—Well, it belongs to Pedro Páramo now. No doubt he's made it happen. Hasn't don Fulgor come to see you?

—No.

—I'm sure he'll be by tomorrow. Or, if not tomorrow, some-day soon.

—Well, he's gonna have to kill me or die trying, but I won't let him get away with this.

—Requiescat in pace, amen, brother-in-law. Just in case.

—You'll see me around, just wait. No need to worry about me. My mother didn't tan my hide all those times for nothing, that's how she made me tough.

—I'll see you tomorrow then. But tell Felicitas I won't be coming for dinner. I wouldn't want to have to tell everyone later: "I was with him the night before he died."

—We'll save something for you in case you change your mind at the last minute.

The thud of footsteps, mixed with the clanking of spurs, was heard as he headed off.

—. . . **TOMORROW, AT DAWN**, you're coming with me, Chona. I've got the animals ready.

—And what if my father loses his temper and dies? As old as he is . . . I'd never forgive myself if something happened to him because of me. I'm the only one he's got who makes sure he takes care of himself. There's nobody else. Why are you in such a hurry to steal me away? Hold off a bit. It won't be long before he's no longer with us.

—You said the same thing last year when you claimed you'd had enough. You even made fun of me back then for being unwilling to take a chance. But this time I've got the mules ready. So, are you coming with me?

—Let me think about it.

—Chona! You have no idea how much I want you. I can't wait any longer. You've just got to come with me.

—Let me think about it. Try to understand. We just need to wait for him to die. He doesn't have much time left. Then I'll go with you, and we won't have to sneak away.

—You said that last year as well.

—So?

—I had to hire the mules. And they're here now. Just waiting for you. Let him take care of himself! You're good-looking. And young. There's got to be some old woman who'd come take care of him. This place is loaded with kind souls.

—I can't.

—Sure you can.

—I can't. You know I'd feel terrible, right? He's my father, after all.

—Then there's nothing else to say. I'll go see Juliana. She's crazy about me.

—Okay then. I won't stand in your way.

—Don't you want to see me tomorrow?

—No. I never want to see you again.

SOUNDS. VOICES. WHISPERINGS. Singing off in the distance:

> *My girl gave me a tissue*
> *with edges made for crying . . .*

In falsetto. As if it were women who were singing.

I SAW CARTS PASSING BY. Oxen lumbering along. Rocks groaning beneath the wheels. Men carried along as if asleep.

«. . . *Every morning the town shudders with passing carts. They come from all over, loaded down with saltpeter, with ears of corn, with hay. Their wheels creak, making the windows rattle, waking everyone. At that same hour, the ovens open and everything smells of freshly baked bread. Suddenly, the sky thunders. Rain falls. Perhaps spring is on its way. When you're there you'll get used to all the "suddenlies," my Son.*»

Empty wagons stirring up the silence of the streets. Disappearing down the dark road of the night. And shadows. The echo of shadows.

I thought about going back. Up above me I could still sense the path I'd followed, like an open wound cutting through the pitch black of the hills.

Then someone touched me on the shoulder.

—What're you doing here?

—I came looking for . . . —and I was about to say who, when I stopped myself— I came looking for my father.

—Why don't you come in?

I went in. It was a house whose roof had half fallen in. Tiles on the ground. The roof on the ground. And in the other half of the house, a man and a woman.

—Are you not dead? —I asked.

The woman smiled. The man stared at me sternly.

—He's drunk —the man said.

—He's just scared —said the woman.

There was a petroleum lamp. A bed made of otate reeds and an equipal chair where the woman's clothes were draped. She was completely naked, the way God sent her into the world. He was as well.

—We heard someone moaning and banging his head against the door. And there you were. What's happened to you?

—So much has happened to me that all I want to do is sleep.

—We were already asleep.

—Then let's get back to sleep.

MY MEMORIES BEGAN TO FADE as morning approached. Now and then I heard the sound of words, and I noticed a difference. Because the words I had heard up to that moment, as

· · · · · · · · · · ·

I was beginning to understand, had no sound, they were silent. You could feel them, but they made no sound, like words you hear in a dream.

—Who could he be? —the woman asked.

—Who knows —the man answered.

—How could he have gotten here?

—Who knows.

—I think I heard him say something about his father.

—I heard him say that as well.

—Could he be lost? Remember when those people showed up claiming to be lost. They were looking for a place called Los Confines, and you told them you had no idea where that was.

—Sure, I remember, but let me sleep. The sun's still not up.

—It will be soon. The reason I'm talking to you is so you'll wake up. You asked me to rouse you before dawn. That's what I'm doing. So get up!

—And why do you want me to get up?

—I don't know why. Last night you told me to wake you. You didn't tell me why.

—In that case, let me sleep. Didn't you hear what that guy said when he arrived? That we should let him sleep. It was the one thing he said.

The voices seem to be fading. Seem to be losing their sound. As if suffocating. Now no one's saying a thing. It's all in my dream.

But soon after, they start up again:

—He just stirred. Perhaps he's wanting to wake up. And if he sees us here, he's gonna ask us things.

—What things could he ask us?

—Well, he'll say something, don't you think?

—Leave him be. He's got to be awfully tired.

—You think so?

—Be quiet, woman.

—Look, he's moving. See how he's trembling? As if something were shaking him from the inside. I know because it's happened to me.

—What's happened to you?

—The same thing.

—I have no idea what you're talking about.

—I wouldn't have said anything if his shaking hadn't reminded me of what I felt the first time you did that thing. And how much it hurt, and how much shame it made me feel.

—What thing do you mean?

—How I felt right after you did it to me, and how I knew it was wrong, even if you say otherwise.

—You're gonna bring that up again? Why don't you go back to sleep and let me do the same?

—You asked me to wake you. And that's what I'm doing. For God's sake, I'm just doing what you wanted. Get moving! It's getting to be time for you to get up.

—Leave me be, woman.

The man seemed to sleep. The woman kept grumbling, but with a very quiet voice:

—It's got to be morning because there's light. I can see that man from here, and if I can see him, that must mean there's light enough to see him. The sun will be up soon. That's a given. If you ask me, that one's up to no good. And we've taken him in. Doesn't matter if it was just for one night, we still let him hide out here. That's going to catch up with us sooner or later . . . Notice how he's tossing and turning, as if he can't get comfortable. If you ask me, something's weighing on his soul.

The morning was growing lighter. The day prevailing over the shadows, pulling them apart. The room where I was felt warm from the heat of sleeping bodies. The dawn filtered through my closed eyelids. I felt the light. I heard:

—He's tossing and turning as if he were cursed. Everything about him suggests he's a bad person. Get up, Donis! Look at him. He's rolling around on the ground, twisting himself all up. Drooling. He's got to be someone who's caused a lot of death. And you didn't notice.

—He's probably just some unfortunate soul. Now go back to sleep and let us rest!

—And how can I sleep if I'm not tired?

—Then get up and find a place where you won't keep bothering me!

—Okay then. I'll go light the fire. And while I'm at it, I'll tell whoever that is to come lay down next to you, in this spot I'm leaving for him.

—Go ahead and tell him.

—I couldn't. It'd scare me to death.

—Then go get your work done and leave us be.

—That's what I'm doing.

—Then what're you waiting for?

—I'm going.

I felt the woman climb out of bed. Her bare feet struck against the floor and passed over my head. I opened my eyes and closed them again.

When I awoke, I felt the midday sun. Beside me, some coffee. I tried to drink. I took a few sips.

—That's all we have. Sorry there's not more. We're short on everything, so short . . .

It was a woman's voice.

—Don't worry about me —I told her—. No need to worry about me. I'm used to it. How can I get out of here?

—Where are you going?

—Anywhere.

—There's a multitude of roads. There's one that goes to Contla, another that returns from there. Another one makes its way straight for the mountains. And the one you see from here, I have no idea where it goes —and she pointed with her finger toward the hole in the ceiling, right where part of the roof had fallen in—. The one over this way runs past the Media Luna. And then there's another one that extends the entire length of the earth. It's the one that travels the farthest.

—Maybe that's the road I came on.

—Where does it go?

—To Sayula.

—You're kidding. And I thought Sayula was over this way. I always wanted to go there. I hear lots of people live there, right?

—About as many as anywhere.

—You don't say. And we're out here all by ourselves. Dying to know anything about life.

—Where'd your husband go?

—He's not my husband. He's my brother, although he doesn't want anyone to know it. Where'd he go? I think he's out looking for a stray calf that's wandering about. At least that's what he told me.

—How long have you two been here?

—Since forever. We were born here.

—You must've known Dolores Preciado.

—Maybe he did, Donis, that is. I know so little about people. I never go anywhere. Right here where you see me now, I've been here sempiternally . . . Well, perhaps not forever. Just since Donis made me his wife. Since then, I've spent all my time shut up in here, seeing as I'm afraid someone might see me. He doesn't want to accept it, but don't you think I'd startle people? —and she moved into the sunlight—. Look at my face!

It was a common face, just like any other.

—What is it you want me to see?

—Don't you see my sin? Don't you see the purplish stains that look like a rash and that cover me from top to bottom? And that's just on the outside, on the inside I'm a sea of mud.

—But who would even see you when there's no one around? I just walked through town and didn't see anyone.

—It might seem so, but there are still a few people. Filomeno is still alive, isn't he? Or what about Dorotea, or Melquiades, or Prudencio the elder, or Sóstenes? Aren't they all still alive? It's just that they don't come out. I have no idea what they do during the day, but at night they shut themselves in. Nights around here are filled with shadows. If only you could see the horde of souls that roam the streets. They come out as soon as it gets dark, and we're all afraid of seeing them. With so many of them and so few of us we no longer plead for them to be freed from their torment. There just aren't enough prayers to go around. Maybe we could say a few lines of the Lord's Prayer for each one, but what good would that do? And then there's the matter of our own sins. There's not a one of us still alive who enjoys the grace of God. We can't even look toward Heaven without feeling our eyes soiled with shame. And shame won't heal anyone. At least that's what the bishop who passed through performing confirmations some time ago told me. I stood right in front of him and confessed everything:

»—Such a thing cannot be forgiven —he told me.

»—I feel so ashamed.

»—That's no remedy.

»—Marry us!

»—Go your separate ways!

»I tried telling him that life had brought us together, had cornered us and forced us into each other's arms. We felt so alone here, being the only ones around. And somehow, we needed to populate the town. Maybe when he returns, there'll be someone here for him to confirm.

»—Leave him. That's all that can be done.

»—But how will we live?

»—As anyone does.

»And he rode off on his mule, his face hardened, without looking back, as if he were fleeing perdition itself. He's never returned. And that's why this place is so full of spirits, a constant movement of restless souls who died without forgiveness and who have no chance of finding it, even less so if they're depending on us. He's coming. Do you hear him?»

—Yes, I hear him.

—It's him.

The door opened.

—How'd it go with the calf? —she asked.

—It wasn't in the mood to come back just now, but I followed its tracks, and I'm close to knowing where it is. I'll get it later tonight.

—You're going to leave me alone at night?

—I might.

—I couldn't bear that. I need you here with me. That's the only time I feel at ease. At night.

—Tonight I'm going after the calf.

—I just found out —I joined in— that you two are brother and sister.

—You just found out? I've known a lot longer than you. So it's best you mind your own business. We don't like people talking about us.

—I only mention it to let you know I understand. No other reason.

—What exactly do you understand?

She placed herself by his side, leaned on his shoulders and repeated:

—What exactly do you understand?

—Nothing —I responded—. With each moment, I understand less and less —then I added—: I just want to go back where I came from. I'll make use of what little bit of light is left in this day.

—It's best to wait —the man said—. Hold off till morning. It'll be dark soon and all the roads are overgrown with brush. You might get lost. I'll show you the way in the morning.

—All right.

THROUGH THE HOLE in the roof, I watched flocks of thrushes pass overhead, those birds that flutter about in the late afternoon just before darkness closes the roads. Then, a few clouds already scattered by the breeze that emerges to usher out the day.

The evening star appeared after that, followed by the moon.

The man and the woman were not there with me. They had gone out through the patio door and by the time they returned night had fallen. As such, they had no idea what had happened while they were gone.

And this is what took place:

Coming in from the street, a woman entered the room. She was old, so very old, and so thin it seemed as if her leathery skin had shriveled tightly around her body. She examined the room with big round eyes. Maybe she saw me. Perhaps she thought I was asleep. She headed straight for the bed and retrieved a trunk from beneath it. She rummaged through it. She tucked some sheets under her arm and tiptoed out as if trying not to wake me.

I kept completely still, holding my breath, trying to look away. But after a while I managed to turn my head in her direction, toward where the evening star was now shining right next to the moon.

—Drink this! —I heard.

I didn't dare move my head again.

—Drink it! It'll do you good. It's orange blossom water. I can tell you're frightened because you're trembling. This will help ease your fear.

I recognized the hands, and when I raised my head, I recognized the face. The man, standing behind her, asked:

—Are you feeling sick?

—I don't know. I see people and things I don't think others can see. A woman was just here. You must've watched her leave.

—Let's go —he told the woman—. Let him be. He must be a mystic.

—We ought to lay him on the bed. Look how he's shaking. He's got to have a fever.

—Don't listen to him. These people get themselves all worked up just for the attention. I met one of them over at the Media Luna who claimed to be clairvoyant. What he failed to foresee was that he was gonna die as soon as the patrón divined his deceit. This guy here must be one of those same mystics. They spend their lives traveling from town to town just "to see what Providence has in store for them." But around here he won't find a single person who'd give him so much as a bite to eat. Notice how he's stopped trembling. Probably because he's listening to what we're saying.

AS IF TIME had turned backwards. I saw the star next to the moon once more. The clouds breaking apart. The flocks of thrushes. And then suddenly the afternoon sky still full of light.

The walls reflecting the afternoon sun. My footsteps sounding against the cobblestones. The muleteer telling me: "Look for doña Eduviges, if she's still alive!"

Then a darkened room. A woman snoring at my side. I noticed that her breathing was uneven, as if she were dreaming, or as if she weren't sleeping at all, but rather imitating the sounds that come with sleep. The bed was made of otate reeds and covered with burlap sacks that smelled of urine, as if they'd never been aired out in the sun. The pillow was an old rag wrapped around some pochote tree fibers or a piece of wool so full of sweat it had become as stiff as a log.

I could feel the woman's naked legs against my knees, and her breath next to my face. I sat up in bed, supporting myself against the pillow that felt like an adobe brick.

—You're not asleep? —she asked.

—I'm not tired. I slept all day. Where's your brother?

—He's out there somewhere. You heard him say he needed to go out. Might not be back tonight.

—So he left all the same? Even when you didn't want him to?

—Yes. And he might not return. That's how it began with everyone else who left. I'm just going over here, I'm just going over there. Until they ended up so far away it was easier not to come back. He's been trying to leave for some time, and I wonder if it might be his turn. Maybe he didn't say so, but he's chosen this moment to take off so you'll stay and take care of me. He saw his chance. The runaway calf was just an excuse. You'll see, he's not coming back.

I wanted to tell her: "I'm going outside for a bit of air. I feel sick." Instead, I said:

—Don't worry. He'll be back.

When I got up, she said:

—I left something for you on the coals in the kitchen. It's not much, but maybe it'll ease your hunger.

I found a few tortillas warming on the coals and a piece of dried meat.

—It's what I was able to get you —I heard her say from over there—. I traded with my sister for two clean sheets I've been keeping from when my mother was still alive. She must've dropped by to pick them up. I didn't want to say anything in front of Donis, but she's the woman who gave you such a fright when you saw her earlier.

A black sky, filled with stars. And next to the moon the largest star of them all.

—DON'T YOU HEAR ME? —I asked in a low voice.

And her voice responded:

—Where are you?

—I'm here, in your town. With your people. Don't you see me?

—No, Son, I don't see you.

Her voice seemed to come from everywhere. Then it disappeared somewhere beyond the limits of the earth.

—I don't see you.

I WENT BACK to that part of the house where half the roof was missing and where that woman was sleeping and told her:

—I'll stay here in this same corner. After all, the bed's just as hard as the floor. Let me know if you need anything.

She responded:

—Donis isn't coming back. I could see it in his eyes. He was just waiting for someone to show up so he could take off. Now it'll fall on you to look after me. Or don't you want to do that? Come sleep next to me.

—I'm fine where I am.

—You'd be better off up here on the bed. The turicatas are gonna eat you alive down there.

So I went and lay beside her.

THE HEAT WOKE ME right about midnight. And the sweat. The body of that woman, formed out of dirt, wrapped in layers of earth, was breaking apart as if it were melting into a puddle of mud. I felt myself swimming in the sweat that poured off her, and I couldn't find any air to breathe. So I got up. The woman was still asleep. A gurgling sound was coming from her mouth, quite like a death rattle.

I headed out onto the street looking for air, but the heat chased after me and wouldn't leave me alone.

And it's because there wasn't any air, just a silent, listless night smoldering in the dog days of August.

There wasn't any air. I had to gulp down the same air that was trying to leave my mouth, grabbing it with both hands before it could escape.

I could feel it flowing out and in, each time a bit thinner, until it became so fine that it seeped through my fingers and disappeared forever.

And I do mean forever.

I recall having seen something like foamy clouds swirling above my head before plunging into that foam and losing myself in its billowy mass. That was the last thing I saw.

—**YOU EXPECT ME** to believe you died of suffocation, Juan Preciado? I found you in the plaza, a long way from Donis's house, and he was right there with me, telling me you were playing dead. Between the two of us, we dragged you into the shade of the portico, already good and stiff, twisted up like someone who's died of fright. If there hadn't been air to breathe the night you're talking about, we wouldn't have had the strength to carry you, let alone lay you to rest. But as you can see, we did bury you.

—You're right, Doroteo. Didn't you say your name was Doroteo?

—It's all the same. Although my name is Dorotea. But it's all the same.

—It's true, Dorotea. It was the murmuring that killed me.

«*You'll find my sanctuary there. The place I most loved. Where I grew dizzy from an abundance of hopes and dreams. My town, rising from the plain. Filled with trees and leaves, like a chest where we've stored our memories. You'll understand why someone there might want to live forever. Dawn, morning, midday, and night, always the same, except for changes in the air. The air alters the color of things, breezes refresh your soul as if life were a passing murmur, as if it were nothing more than a soft murmuring . . .*»

—Yes, Dorotea. It was the murmuring that killed me. Even though I'd worked to control my fear. All the same, it kept building until I could bear it no more. And when I found myself surrounded by all that whispering, that's when my last thread of sanity broke.

«I made it to the plaza, you're right about that. I was drawn there by the noise of so many people I imagined were actually there. By then I was no longer in my right mind. I remember making my way by holding myself up against the walls, as if I were walking with my hands. The murmuring seemed to seep from the walls as if filtering through the cracks and the missing mortar. I heard them. They were human voices, but not clear ones, muted, as if they were whispering something to me as I passed, like a droning in my ears. I moved away from the walls and continued down the middle of the street, but I heard them all the same, as if they were traveling with me, whether in front or behind. I no longer felt the heat I mentioned earlier. Instead, I was cold. From the moment I left the house of the woman who'd shared her bed with me and who, as I said, I'd watched disintegrate in the moisture of her own sweat, ever since then I'd felt a penetrating cold. As I walked, the chill got worse, until goosebumps covered my skin. I wanted to turn back, thinking I might try to find the warmth I'd left behind. But after a while I began to understand that the cold was coming from inside me, from my own blood. That's when I realized I was terrified. I heard the commotion coming from the plaza, and I imagined that being among all those people might calm my fear. That's why the two of you found me in the plaza. So Donis came back after all? That woman was sure she'd never see him again.»

—It was morning by the time we found you. I'm not sure where he was coming from. I didn't ask.

—Anyway, I made it to the plaza. I leaned against one of the pillars of the portico. I saw that no one was there, though I could still hear murmuring that sounded like a crowd of people on market day. A steady commotion, without rhyme or reason, like the sound made by the wind as it beats against the branches of a tree at night. And even though you don't see the tree or the branches, you hear them rustling. Something like that. I didn't take another step. I began to feel the whispering getting closer, buzzing around me like a swarm of bees, until finally I could make out a few words that were almost devoid of sound: "Pray to God for us." That's what I heard them saying. And that's when my soul froze over. And that's why you found me dead.

—It would've been better had you never left home. Why'd you come?

—I told you at the beginning. I came looking for Pedro Páramo, who seems to have been my father. It was that hope that brought me here.

—Hope? You pay dearly for that. It was that type of illusion that made me live longer than I should have. That's the price I paid for hoping to find my son, who, as it turns out, was nothing more than a longing, since I never really had a son. Now that I'm dead, I've had time to think and to understand everything. God didn't grant me so much as a nest to raise a child in. Just a long, drawn-out life during which my sorrowful eyes searched here and there, always a bit askance, as if to see around all the people I suspected might have hidden my son from me. And it was all on account of a bad dream. I've had two dreams: one I call my "blessed" dream, the other my "cursed" one. The first was the one that made me imagine I had a child. And while I was alive, I never stopped believing it to be true because I could feel him in my arms, so tender, with his little mouth and eyes and hands. For the longest time I could feel on the tips of my fingers the outline of his eyes as he slept and the beating of his heart. Why wouldn't I suppose it was true? I carried him with me wherever I went, wrapped in my rebozo; and then, suddenly, he was gone. In Heaven, they told me they had made a mistake. That they had given me the heart of a mother, but the womb of a harlot. Then this was the other dream I had. I got to Heaven and looked around to see if I might recognize my child's countenance among the angels. But nothing. All the faces were the same, cast from the same mold. So I asked. One of those saints came over and, without saying a word, buried one of his hands in my gut as if he had buried it in a ball of wax. When he pulled it out, he showed me something that looked a bit like a nutshell. "Take this as proof of what you are being shown."

»You know the strange way they speak up there, but you understand them. I wanted to explain how that thing was just my stomach all shriveled from hunger and so little use, but another one of those saints grabbed me by the shoulders and pushed me toward the door: "Go rest on earth a while longer, my daughter. And try to be good to lessen your time in Purgatory."

»That was my "cursed" dream, and it's the one that made me realize I had never had a son. That understanding came quite late, after my body had shrunk, after my spine had bent over forcing my head down, after I could no longer walk. Moreover, the town was becoming deserted. Everyone took off in different directions, taking with them the charity that kept me alive. I sat down to wait for death. After we found you, my bones were determined to find some rest. "Nobody'll even notice me," I thought. I'm not enough of anything to bother anyone. And you see, I didn't even need my own space here in the ground. They buried me in your grave, tucked away in the hollow of your arms. Here in this tiny little nook where I am now. Although it occurs to me that I should be the one holding you in my arms. You hear that? It's raining up there. Don't you feel the rain beating down?»

—It feels as if someone were walking on top of us.

—It's time to stop being terrified. No one can scare you anymore. Try to think pleasant thoughts, seeing as we're going to be buried a long while here in the ground.

AT DAWN, THICK DROPS of rain fell over the earth. They made a hollow sound as they hit against the soft, loose dirt of the furrows. A mockingbird flew just above the ground, howling as if imitating a child's lament. As the bird got farther away it moaned as if weary, and when it was more distant still, where the horizon was beginning to open up, it let out a hiccup, then a good laugh, followed by another moan.

Fulgor Sedano took notice of the fresh smell of earth and looked outside to watch as rain penetrated the furrows. His tiny eyes gleamed with delight. He took three deep breaths, savoring the sensation, and he smiled broadly, showing his teeth.

«Good Lord! —he said—. Another great year.» Then he added: "Fall, sweet rain, fall. And keep coming till you're exhausted! Then head over that way. Remember that we've worked hard to turn the soil, just for you, for your pleasure."

And he chuckled.

Returning from its flight around the fields, the mockingbird crossed in front of him and let out an anguished howl.

The rain began spilling from the clouds with greater intensity until, off in the distance, over where the sun had started to rise, the sky closed back up, and the night that was beginning to recede seemed to return.

The main gate at the Media Luna groaned as it swung open, soaked by the wet breeze. Two men rode out, then two more, then another two, until as many as two hundred men on horseback had scattered across the rain-soaked fields.

—We need to drive the cattle from the Enmedio Ranch past what used to be the Estagua Ranch, and run the herd at the Estagua Ranch up to the Vilmayo hills —ordered Fulgor Sedano as they headed out—. And be quick about it, the rain's gonna hit us hard!

He repeated the same instruction so many times that the last men to leave had only heard: "From here to there and from there even farther."

Each man lifted a hand to his sombrero to signal he had understood.

The last one had barely left when Miguel Páramo appeared at a full gallop and, without slowing, swung down from his horse, almost landing on top of Fulgor, letting his mount make its own way back to the stable.

—Where're you coming from this time of day, young man?

—I've been out milking.

—Milking who?

—Can't you guess?

—Must be Dorotea, La Cuarraca. Round here, she's the only one who likes babies.

—You're an idiot, Fulgor, but that's not your fault.

And without removing his spurs, he took off in search of someone to get him some breakfast.

In the kitchen, Damiana Cisneros asked him the same question.

—Where've you been, Miguel?

—Out and about, checking in on your mother.

—No need to get mad. Forget I asked. How should I cook your eggs?

—However turns you on.

—I wasn't being vulgar, Miguel.

—I know, Damiana. Forget what I said. Hey, do you know a woman named Dorotea, the one they call La Cuarraca?

—I do. And if you want to see her, she's right outside. She gets up early every morning and swings by here for some breakfast. She's the one always walking around with a bundle in her rebozo, cooing to it and telling everyone it's her baby. Something bad must've happened to her back in the day, but since she never talks no one really knows what it was. She survives on whatever people give her.

—Damn that old man Fulgor! I'm gonna teach him a lesson that'll make his head spin.

But then he wondered if that woman might not prove useful. And without hesitation, he went to the back door of the kitchen and called to Dorotea:

—Come here. I've got a proposition for you —he told her.

Who knows what type of deal he might have offered her, the only thing certain is that when he came back inside, he was rubbing his hands together:

—Bring on those eggs! —he shouted to Damiana, adding—: From now on you'll let that woman eat whatever I'm having, even if it kills your stingy self to do so.

Meanwhile, Fulgor Sedano headed out to the granary to check the level of the corn. He was worried about how much was being used since the harvest was still some way off. In fact, they had just barely finished planting. "I need to see if this will last us." Then he added: "That boy! Just like his old man, but he's starting off too soon. At this rate, I can't imagine he's gonna survive. I forgot to tell him some people came by yesterday accusing him of having killed a man. If he keeps this up . . ."

He let out a deep breath and tried to imagine where the ranch hands would be headed by now. But he was distracted by Miguel Páramo's sorrel, which was rubbing its muzzle against the fence. "He hasn't even taken its saddle off," he thought. "Nor will he. At least don Pedro is more reliable and even has moments when he's calm. But he sure coddles that Miguel. Yesterday when I told him what his son had done, he responded: 'Let's just tell people I'm the one responsible, Fulgor. He couldn't have done it, he's not yet man enough to kill someone. To do something like that, he'd need balls this big.' He held his hands up, as if he were showing the size of a pumpkin. 'Anything he does, put the blame on me.'"

—Miguel's gonna cause you a lot of headaches, don Pedro. He likes getting in trouble.

—Give him some space. He's just a kid. How old is he now? Must be seventeen. Right, Fulgor?

—Could be. I remember when they brought him to us as a newborn, seems like yesterday. But he's so violent and always in such a hurry, sometimes it feels like he's racing against time. He's gonna lose that race, you'll see.

—He's still a baby, Fulgor.

—Whatever you say, don Pedro, but the woman who came by yesterday sobbing, claiming that son of yours killed her husband, was beyond hysterical. I know how to size up a person's grief, don Pedro. And that woman was bursting at the seams with it. I offered her fifty hectoliters of corn if she'd forget the whole thing, but she wouldn't take it. So I promised her we'd settle the matter some other way. She still wasn't satisfied.

—Who were those people?

—People I don't know.

—Then don't worry about it, Fulgor. Those people don't exist.

He made it to the granary and felt the warmth of the corn. He grabbed a handful to make sure weevils hadn't gotten into it. He measured the height: "This'll do —he said—. As soon as the grass starts growing, we won't have to keep giving corn to the livestock. There's more than enough."

On the way back, he looked up at the sky full of clouds: "We'll have rain for a good while yet." And he forgot about everything else.

—THE WEATHER UP THERE must be changing. My mother always said that as soon as it began to rain everything would fill with light and the verdant smell of new growth. She talked about how the clouds would roll in, about how they would toss themselves to the ground, shattering the earth and changing its colors . . . My mother, who spent her childhood here in this town, as well as the best years of her life, and yet was unable to return here to die. So she had me come in her place. It's strange, Dorotea, how I never even got to see the sky. At least that, perhaps, hasn't changed from the way she knew it.

—I wouldn't know, Juan Preciado. It's been so long since I lifted my head, I've forgotten about the heavens. And even if I had looked up, what good would it've done me? The sky is so far up there, and my eyes so feeble, I was content just knowing where the ground was. Besides, I lost all interest in looking up when Father Rentería assured me I'd never know the Glory of God. Said I wouldn't get to see it even from a distance . . . On account of my sins. But he shouldn't have told me that. Life beats you down all on its own. The only thing that keeps a person going is the hope you'll end up someplace different after you die, but when one door slams in your face and the only other one takes you straight to Hell, it would've been better never to have been born . . . For me, Juan Preciado, Heaven is right here where I am now.

—And what about your soul? Where do you think it's disappeared to?

—I suspect it's wandering the earth like so many others, searching for anyone still alive who'll pray for it. It's possible it despises me for the way I treated it, but I no longer care. I've broken free of its obsessive need for remorse. It turned bitter what little food I was able to eat, and it made my nights unbearable by filling them with terrifying visions of the damned and that sort of thing. When I sat down to die, it begged me to get back up to keep dragging out my life, as if it still hoped for some miracle that might cleanse my sins. I didn't even try: "This is the end of the road —I told it—. I don't have the strength to keep going." I opened my mouth to let it escape. And it took off. I felt it when the delicate thread of blood that still joined it to my heart dropped into my hands.

THEY KNOCKED AT HIS DOOR, but he didn't answer. He listened as they knocked on all the doors, waking everyone up. Fulgor —he recognized him by his gait— was rushing toward the main door but paused for just a moment as if intending to knock again. But then he kept running.

Whispered voices. Slow dragging of footsteps, as if someone were carrying something heavy.

Indistinct noises.

The memory of his father's death stirred in his mind. Then, like now, it was the break of day, although on that occasion the door was already open, letting the gray hue of a forlorn and ashen sky filter in. A woman holding back her tears leaning against the door. A mother whom he had forgotten, forgotten so many times before, telling him: "They've killed your father!" In a broken, defeated voice, barely held together by the thread of her wailing.

He never liked reliving that memory since it brought on others, as if he had torn a hole in a bag full of grain and was struggling to hold back the contents. The death of his father had been followed by so many other deaths, and with each one he saw the same vision of his father's face ripped open, one eye shattered, the other looking on vengefully. And that memory came back again and then again, until he had wiped it from his mind, but only when there was no one left to remind him of it.

—Lay him down here! No, not like that. With his head back that way. You! What're you waiting for?

All in hushed voices.

—And him?

—He's asleep. Don't wake him. Don't make any noise.

He just stood there, enormous, watching the men working to lay out a bundle wrapped in old burlap sacks and strapped together with lashing cord as if wound in a shroud.

—Who is it? —he asked.

Fulgor Sedano approached him and said:

—It's Miguel, don Pedro.

—What'd they do to him? —he yelled.

He was expecting to hear: "They killed him." And he was already working to hold back the rage that was balling up in the pit of his stomach when he heard Fulgor Sedano respond gently:

—No one did anything to him. He found death all by himself.

Petroleum lamps kept the night at bay.

—. . . His horse killed him —someone added.

They went to lay him out on his bed. They pushed the mattress to the floor, exposing the bare boards, and there they positioned the body that was now free of the straps they had used to carry it. They placed his hands on his chest and covered his face with a black cloth. "He seems bigger now than he was," Fulgor Sedano muttered under his breath.

Pedro Páramo stood there without showing emotion, as if he were someplace else. His thoughts chased around in his head, unable to come to any conclusion or understanding. Finally, he said:

—I'm beginning to pay. Better to start early, to finish sooner.

He felt no grief.

And when he spoke up to thank those who had gathered in the patio, he found just enough strength and chose just the right words for his voice to push its way through the commotion of wailing women. Later that night, the only sound anyone could hear was that of Miguel Páramo's sorrel pawing at the ground.

—Tomorrow —he ordered Fulgor Sedano— send someone to put that animal out of its misery.

—Sure thing, don Pedro. Understood. The poor thing must be heartbroken.

—I agree, Fulgor. And while you're at it, tell those women to stop making such a fuss, it's too much racket for a death that belongs to me. If it'd been one of their own, I'm sure they wouldn't be bawling with so much enthusiasm.

MANY YEARS LATER, Father Rentería would recall the night the hardness of his bed kept him awake, eventually forcing him to head outside. It was the night Miguel Páramo died.

He wandered Comala's lonely streets, his footsteps scaring off dogs that were sniffing through the garbage. He made it as far as the river, where he passed the time gazing at still pools of water that reflected the light of stars falling from the heavens.

He stayed several hours, wrestling with his thoughts and tossing them into the black water of the river.

«This all began —he thought— when Pedro Páramo, coming from such low beginnings, climbed his way to the top. He grew like a weed. The worst part is I made it all possible: "I confess Father that last night I slept with Pedro Páramo." "I confess Father that I had a son by Pedro Páramo." "That I gave my daughter to Pedro Páramo." I kept waiting for him to show up and confess something himself, but he never did. And then through that son of his, he widened the range of his depravity. The only son he chose to recognize, only God knows why. What I do know is that I placed that instrument in his hands.»

He remembered well the day he had taken Miguel to him as a newborn.

He had told him:

—Don Pedro, the mother died giving birth. Said he was yours. Here he is.

And without hesitation, he merely responded:

—Why don't you keep him, Father? Make him a priest.

—Not with the blood that runs through his veins. I don't want that responsibility.

—You really think I have bad blood?

—I really do, don Pedro.

—I'll prove you wrong. Leave him here. There are plenty of people who'll take care of him.

—That's what I figured. At least with you he'll have what he needs to survive.

The child, tiny as it was, wiggled about like a serpent.

—Damiana! Come take care of this thing. It's my son.

After that he cracked open a bottle:

—Here's to the late mother, and to you.

—And to the infant?

—To him as well, why not?

He poured another glass and both men drank to the future of the little one.

That's how it all began.

Oxcarts began rolling by on their way to the Media Luna. He ducked down, hiding behind the embankment along the river. "Who are you hiding from?" he asked himself.

—Adiós, Father! —he heard one of the cart drivers say.

He stood up and answered:

—Adiós! May the Lord bless you.

Gradually, the lights around town were being put out. The river let loose a stream of vibrant colors.

—Have they already rung the first bell, Father? —one of the other drivers asked.

—It must be long past the first bell —he responded. And he walked in the opposite direction not wanting to be held up.

—Where you off to so early, Father?

—Who's dying, Father?

—Has someone died in Contla, Father?

He would've liked to have answered: "Me, I'm the one who's died." But he settled for a smile.

As he left town, he picked up his pace.

It was late in the morning by the time he made it back.

—Where've you been, Uncle? —his niece Ana asked—. A whole bunch of women came looking for you. They were hoping to confess today, since tomorrow is First Friday.

—They can come back this evening.

He rested a while on one of the benches in the hallway, overcome with fatigue.

—The air is so refreshing, isn't it, Ana?

—It's hot, Uncle.

—I don't feel it.

He had no desire whatsoever to think about how he'd just been to Contla to make a general confession, and the priest, despite his pleas, had refused to give him absolution:

—That man you refuse to mention by name has torn your Church apart, and you've allowed him to do it. What should we expect from you now, Father? What have you accomplished with the authority of God? I want to convince myself you're a good man and that the people there hold you in high esteem, but it's not enough to be good. Sin is wrong. And to get rid of it, you have to be tough, even ruthless. I would love to believe your congregants are all still believers, but it's not you who keeps their faith alive. They do that on their own, through superstition and fear. I so want to stand with you in the poverty in which you live and acknowledge the effort you exhibit every day while fulfilling your obligations. I fully understand how hard our mission is in these wretched little towns where they've stashed us away; but that knowledge gives me the right to remind you that we cannot impart our service only to the privileged few, to the ones who offer a pittance in exchange for your soul. And with your soul in their possession what hope do you have of prevailing over those who are better than you? No, Father, my hands are not sufficiently clean to grant you absolution. You'll have to find that somewhere else.

—Do you mean to tell me, Father, that I need to go elsewhere to confess my sins?

—You need to go someplace else. You cannot continue consecrating others when you're mired in sin yourself.

—And what if they suspend my ministry?

—I doubt it will come to that, even though it might be what you deserve. That decision lies with them.

—Wouldn't you be able to . . . ? Provisionally, let's say . . . I need to give last rites . . . Communion. So many are dying in my town, Father.

—Father, let the dead be judged by God.

—No, then?

With that, the priest in Contla had refused him.

Later, the two men wandered through the parish corridors, shaded by azaleas. They sat beneath a canopy covered in ripening grapes.

—They're acidic, Father —the priest answered, anticipating the question he was going to ask—. We live in a place where Providence allows everything to grow, but it all ends up bitter. That's our punishment.

—You're right, Father. I've tried to grow grapes over in Comala. They never thrive. The only thing that grows are arrayán and orange trees, both of them bitter. I can't recall what it's like to taste something sweet. Do you remember the Chinese guavas we had in the seminary? The peaches. And those tangerines whose peels would open right up if you gave them a little squeeze. I brought a few seeds with me. Just a few, enough to fill a small bag . . . Later I felt it would've been better to have left them where they could've grown, since bringing them here meant bringing them to die.

—And yet, Father, they say the land around Comala is good. What a shame it's all in the hands of a single man. Is Pedro Páramo still the owner?

—Such is the will of God.

—I doubt God's will has anything to do with it. You don't believe that, do you, Father?

—There are times I've doubted it, but the people of Comala are sure that's the case.

—And do you agree with them?

—I'm just a simple man, willing to humble myself while I still feel the urge to do so.

Later, as they said their goodbyes, he took the priest's hands and kissed them. But now he was back here, back to reality, with absolutely no desire to keep thinking about the morning he had spent in Contla.

He stood up and walked toward the door.

—Where are you going, Uncle?

His niece Ana, always there, always by his side, as if hoping to hide from life while protected by his shadow.

—I'm going for a walk, Ana. To see if I can't shake this off.

—Are you feeling sick?

—Not sick, Ana. Bad. A bad person. That's what I feel I am.

He headed over to the Media Luna and offered his condolences to Pedro Páramo. He listened as that man once again offered regrets for the accusations that had been leveled against his son. He let him say his piece. After all, it no longer mattered. But he did decline his invitation to eat with him:

—I'm sorry, don Pedro. I need to get to the church early, since there are scores of women waiting for me at the confessional. Perhaps some other time.

He walked back slowly, and, as darkness was beginning to fall, he entered the church just as he was, caked in dirt and misery. He took his seat to hear confession.

The first to come forward was the old woman Dorotea, who was always there waiting for the church doors to open.

He noticed that she smelled of alcohol.

—So now you're getting yourself drunk? Since when?

—It's because I was just at Miguelito's wake, Father. And I overdid it a bit. They gave me so much to drink I made a fool of myself.

—You've never been anything else, Dorotea.

—But this time I've brought a lot of sins to confess, Father. Bunches of them.

Time and again he had told her: "Don't come to confession, Dorotea, you're just wasting my time. You couldn't sin anymore, even if you tried. Let others have a chance."

—This time I've sinned for real, Father. It's the truth.

—Tell me.

—Now that I can't hurt him anymore, I can mention that I was the one who got all those girls for the late Miguelito Páramo.

Father Rentería, after stalling for a moment to think, appeared to wake from a trance and asked, almost as a matter of routine:

—Since when?

—Since he was a young fella. Ever since he got the urge.

—Repeat what you just said, Dorotea.

—I said I was the one who got all those girls for Miguelito.

—You took them to him?

—Sometimes I did. Other times I'd just set it up. Then with others I'd merely point him in the right direction. You know, telling him when they'd be all alone so he could take them by surprise.

—Were there many?

He hadn't meant to ask, but the question came out as if by habit.

—So many I lost count. Loads of them.

—What would you have me do with you, Dorotea? Be your own judge. See if you can forgive yourself.

—I can't, Father. But you can. That's why I'm here to see you.

—How many times have you shown up asking me to send you to Heaven when you die? You were hoping to find your son there, right, Dorotea? Well, now you won't be going to Heaven. But may God forgive you anyway.

—Thank you, Father.

—Yes. And I forgive you in His name as well. You may go.

—Aren't you gonna give me any penance?

—None is necessary, Dorotea.

—Thank you, Father.

—Go with God.

He tapped his knuckles on the confessional window to call
the next woman. And as he listened to her words, "Bless me
Father, for I have sinned," his head sank as if it could no longer
hold itself up. Then came dizziness, confusion, and a feeling as
if he were dissolving in thick water; then spinning lights, the
remaining light of day breaking into pieces, and the taste of
blood on his tongue. Then he heard again, "Bless me Father, for
I have sinned," this time more forcefully, then again and again,
followed by: "forever and ever, amen," "forever and ever, amen,"
"forever . . ."

—Hush now —he said—. When was the last time you
confessed?

—Two days ago, Father.

There it was again. As if he were surrounded by misfortune.
"What are you doing here? —he thought to himself—. Rest. Go
and rest. You're exhausted."

He rose from the confessional and headed toward the sacristy.
Without looking back, he said to the people waiting for him:

—Those of you who feel unburdened by sin may receive
Holy Communion tomorrow.

Behind him, the only sound was a soft murmur.

I'M LYING IN the same bed where my mother died years ago,
on the same mattress, under the same black wool blanket we
would wrap ourselves in to fall asleep. In those days, I slept
beside her, in the tiny space she'd open for me between her arms.

I believe I can still feel the slow cadence of her breathing, the
palpitations and sighing that cradled my dreams . . . I believe I
can still feel the grief of her passing . . .

But none of that is true.

I'm in this place now, laid out on my back, remembering
that moment in the past as a way of forgetting my loneliness.

Because I won't be lying here for just a short while. Nor am I in my mother's bed, but in a black box like the ones people use to bury the dead. Because I'm dead.

I sense this place where I find myself, and I ponder . . .

I think about when the limes would ripen. About the winds in February that would snap the fern stalks before they dried out from neglect. About the scent of ripe limes that would fill the old patio.

On February mornings the wind would drop out of the mountains. Meanwhile, the clouds would stay up high, waiting for better weather to entice them down into the valley, leaving the blue sky above empty and allowing the light to drop onto the wind that would spread playfully across the land in circles, stirring up the dirt and rustling the branches of the orange trees.

The sparrows would laugh, pecking at the leaves that the wind pushed to the ground, then they would laugh again. They would abandon feathers among the thorny branches and chase after butterflies and laugh some more. It was that time of year.

February, when the mornings were full of wind, sparrows, and bluish light. I remember.

That's when my mother died.

I should have screamed. I should have rubbed my hands raw out of desperation. That's what you would have wanted. But wasn't that such a pleasant morning? A breeze was blowing through the open door, tearing at the edges of the ivy. Hair was beginning to grow between my legs, and my hands were warm and trembled as they touched my breasts. The sparrows were playing. Wheat was swaying on the hillside. I felt sad thinking she would no longer see the wind frolicking in the jasmine, that her eyes would no longer observe the light of day. But why should I cry?

Do you remember, Justina? You arranged the chairs in the corridor so those coming to see her could wait their turn. They

· · · · · · · · · ·

were all empty. My mother all alone, surrounded by candles;
her face pale, her white teeth just visible through purple lips
stiffened by the chill of death. Her eyelashes motionless, her
heart without life. You and I alone, praying incessantly, although
she heard nothing, we heard nothing, our efforts lost in the noise
of the wind that raged beneath the night. You ironed her black
dress, starching the collar and the cuffs on the sleeves so her
hands would seem young as they lay across her lifeless bosom,
the same worn out and loving bosom where I had slept as a child,
the one that had given me nourishment, and whose pounding
had lulled me to sleep.

No one came to see her. It was better that way. Death is not
shared with others as if it were a blessing. No one goes looking
for sorrow.

Someone knocked at the door. You left.

—You go —I said—. People's faces seem blurry to me. Ask
them to go away. Could they be here to collect the money for the
Gregorian masses? She didn't leave any money. Tell them that,
Justina. Will she end up stuck in Purgatory if no one says those
masses? Who are they to hand out justice, Justina? Do you think
I'm crazy? I don't mind.

And those chairs of yours remained empty until we headed
out to bury her with men hired for their labor, sweating under the
weight of a stranger, and removed from our pain. They shoveled
wet sand into the grave before slowly lowering the coffin, with the
patience of their vocation, standing in a cool breeze that rewarded
their efforts. Their eyes cold, indifferent. They said: "This is the
amount." And you paid them, as you would if you were buying
any old thing, pulling the knot out of your handkerchief that was
damp with tears, that you'd wrung out once and then once again,
and that now held the money for the burial . . .

And when they left, you knelt on the spot where her face had
been, kissed the ground, and you might have dug down toward

her had I not said: "Let's go, Justina, she's somewhere else. The only thing still here is something that's dead."

—WAS THAT YOU saying all that, Dorotea?

—Who, me? I fell asleep for a while. Are they still frightening you?

—I heard someone speaking. A woman's voice. I thought it was you.

—A woman's voice? You thought it was me? It must be the one who talks to herself. The woman in the large sepulcher. Doña Susanita. She's buried here beside us. The moisture must have reached her so she's tossing in her sleep.

—Who's that?

—Pedro Páramo's last wife. Some say she was insane. Others say she wasn't. Truth is, she talked to herself even while she was alive.

—She must have died a long time ago.

—Gosh, yes! A long time ago. What was it you heard her saying?

—Something about her mother.

—But she didn't have a mother . . .

—Well, that's what she was talking about.

—. . . Or at least she didn't bring her along when she came. But wait. I'm remembering now that she was born here but disappeared when she was older. And, yes, her mother died of consumption. She was a strange woman who was always sick and never visited anyone.

—That's what she was saying. That no one went to visit her mother when she died.

—But what's she talking about? Obviously no one came by the house for fear of getting consumption. Could that little brat have remembered all that?

—That's what she was saying.

—Tell me when you hear her again. I'd like to know what she's talking about.

—Hear that? I think she's about to speak. I hear murmuring.

—No, that's not her. That's farther away, and from the other direction. And it's a man's voice. It's just that when moisture reaches these corpses that have already been dead awhile, they begin to stir. And they wake up.

«The Heavens are good. God was with me that night. If not, who knows what might've happened? Because it was already night when I came to . . .»

—Can you hear that better now?

—I can.

«. . . There was blood everywhere. And as I stood up, my hands slipped on rocks that were covered in blood. My blood. Loads of it. And yet I wasn't dead. I could tell I wasn't. It seemed that don Pedro wasn't interested in killing me, just in giving me a fright. He wanted to know if I had been out at Vilmayo two months earlier. On the feast day of San Cristóbal. At the wedding. What wedding? What San Cristóbal? I splashed around in my own blood and asked him: "What wedding, don Pedro?" No, no, don Pedro, I wasn't there. Maybe I passed by there. But only by chance . . . He had no intention of killing me. As you can see, all he did was leave me lame and with one of my arms messed up. But he never killed me. From that moment, people have been telling me one of my eyes is crooked, on account of the scare. Yet I'm convinced I'm more of a man because of it. The Heavens are good. Don't ever doubt that.»

—Who could that be?

—No idea. Could be anybody. After don Lucas was shot, Pedro Páramo caused so much destruction people say he killed off just about everyone who attended the wedding where his father was set to give away the bride. The thing is, don Lucas was killed by mistake, since it seems the real grudge was against the groom. But since they never found out where the bullet that hit him came from, Pedro Páramo went after them all. This happened over on the hill at Vilmayo. There used to be a few ranches up there, but you won't find any trace of them anymore . . . Listen, that sounds like her now. Your ears are younger than mine, so listen close. Then tell me what she says.

—I can't make out a thing. It doesn't seem like she's talking, just grumbling.

—What's she grumbling about?

—Who knows.

—It's got to be about something. Nobody complains about nothing. Listen close.

—She's just complaining, nothing more. Maybe Pedro Páramo made her suffer.

—Don't believe it. He loved her. Take my word for it, he loved her more than any other woman. But by the time they brought her to him she was already suffering and maybe even crazy. He loved her so much he spent his remaining years slumped over in an equipal chair, gazing down the road where they'd carried her off to the cemetery. He lost interest in everything. He abandoned his lands and ordered the equipment burned. Some say he was exhausted, others that he was disillusioned. What's certain is that he ran everyone off and just sat down in that equipal and stared down the road she'd left on.

»From then on, the land was left fallow, as if it were barren. It was disheartening to watch those fields deteriorate as they were hit with all kinds of plagues. People everywhere started to melt away, the men scattering in search of better "watering holes." I remember days when Comala was filled with the sound of "adiós," and we thought it was great fun to go bid farewell to those who were leaving. But only because they were leaving with every intention of coming back. They left their possessions and their families in our care. Later, some of them sent for their families, though not for their things. Eventually they seemed simply to forget about us, about the town, and even about their things. I stuck around since I didn't have anywhere to go. Others stayed waiting for Pedro Páramo to die, because, as they explained, he'd promised to leave everything to them, and based on that hope they stuck around. But year after year rolled by, and he was still alive, always there, watching over the lands of the Media Luna like a scarecrow.

»Then, when he finally was close to death, there was that thing they called the Cristero War that rounded up the few men who were still around. That's when I really began to die of hunger, and I never recovered.

»All because of Pedro Páramo, on account of the torment that filled his soul. All because his wife died, that Susanita. So don't tell me he didn't love her.»

IT WAS FULGOR SEDANO who gave him the news:

—Patrón, want to guess who's back in town?

—Who?

—Bartolomé San Juan.

—What for?

—That's what I want to know. Why's he back?

—You haven't looked into it?

—No. Thought I should tell you first. Thing is, he never asked about a place to stay. He went straight to that old house of yours. He got off his horse and unloaded his suitcases, as if you'd already rented the place to him. At least that's how he acted.

—And what's wrong with you, Fulgor? Shouldn't you have already found out what's going on? Isn't that what you're here for?

—I was just so confused by what I saw. But I'll check things out tomorrow if you think I should.

—Leave tomorrow to me. I'll take care of it. Are they both there?

—Yes. He and his wife. But how'd you know that?

—Wouldn't it be his daughter?

—Considering the way he treats her, it would seem she's his wife.

—Go to bed, Fulgor.

—With your permission.

«**I WAITED THIRTY YEARS** for you to come back, Susana. I waited to have it all. Not just some things, but all things that could be had, so there would be nothing left to desire, except you, only my desire for you. How many times did I plead with your father to come back here to live, saying I needed him? I even misled him.

»I offered to make him my administrator, just so I could see you again. And how did he respond? "No response —the messenger would always say—. Don Bartolomé tears up your letters as soon as I deliver them." But from that boy I learned you'd gotten married. Later, that you'd been widowed and were back living with your father.

»After that, silence.

»Every time my messenger headed out, he'd return saying:

»—I can't find them, don Pedro. Everyone says they left Mascota. Some say they went this way, others say that way.

»And I'd respond:

»—Don't worry about the costs. Keep looking for them. It's not like the earth swallowed them whole.

»Then one day he came to report:

»—I wandered all over those mountains looking for the rock don Bartolomé San Juan was hiding under, and I've finally found him. He's way out there, holed up in a gully on the side of a hill, living in a small shack made of logs, near the abandoned La Andrómeda mines.

»By then strange winds were already blowing. There was talk of men who'd taken up arms. We heard all kinds of rumors. That's what swept your father down out of the mountains. Not for his own sake, as he explained in a letter, but out of concern for your safety. He wanted to bring you someplace with plenty of people.

»It felt as if Heaven was beginning to part. I wanted to run to you. To wrap you in joy. To cry. And I did cry, Susana, when I learned you were finally returning.»

—SOME TOWNS REEK of misfortune. You recognize them with a quick taste of their stale air, which is thin and worn out like all things old. This is one of those towns, Susana.

»At least back where we were before, a person could take pleasure in watching all the things that would spring to life: the clouds, the birds, the moss. Do you remember? But here the only thing you notice is that pungent, yellowish odor that seems to seep out of everything. This is a deplorable little town, slathered in misfortune.

»He asked us to come back. He even lent us his house. He's provided everything we could need. But there's no reason for us to be grateful for any of it. It's bad luck for us to be back here, in this place that will grant us no salvation. I can feel it.

»You know what Pedro Páramo wants from me? I didn't expect the things he has given us would come free of charge. And I was ready to settle up by offering my labor, since I knew we'd have to repay him somehow. I told him all about La Andrómeda and made him see the place has possibilities if you were to make a plan to work it. Know what he said? "I'm not interested in your mine, Bartolomé San Juan. The only thing I want from you is your daughter. She's your best work."

»So, it seems it's you he wants, Susana. Says you played together as kids. That he already knows you. That you even swam together in the river when you were young. I didn't know about any of that; had I known I would have beat you silly.»

—I'm sure you will.

—Did you just say: I'm sure you will?

—I did.

—You mean to tell me you're ready to sleep with him?

—Yes, Bartolomé.

—You know he's married, and he's had any number of women?

—Yes, Bartolomé.

—Don't call me Bartolomé. I'm your father!

Bartolomé San Juan, a dead miner. Susana San Juan, daughter of a miner dead in the Andrómeda mines. He saw it clearly. "I'll have to go there to die," he thought. Then he said:

—I've told him you're still living with your husband even though you're a widow, or at least that's how you act. I've tried to dissuade him, but he scowls when I talk to him, and he shuts his eyes every time your name comes up. As far as I can tell that man is pure evil. That's what Pedro Páramo is.

—And what am I?

—You're my daughter. Mine. The daughter of Bartolomé San Juan.

Thoughts began to stir in Susana San Juan's mind, slowly at first, then holding back, before finally racing so fast she could only say:

—That's not true. It's not true.

—This world grabs onto us so tightly it squeezes out fistfuls of our dust here and there, breaking us into pieces as if to douse

the land with our blood. What did we do? Why have our souls
rotted away? Your mother always said we could at least trust in
God's good graces. Yet that is something you deny. Why would
you say I'm not your father? Have you gone mad?

—Do you really not know?

—Have you gone mad?

—Of course I have, Bartolomé. Did you really not know?

—**DID YOU KNOW**, Fulgor, that she's the most beautiful
woman ever born to this earth? I began to believe I'd lost her
forever. I have no intention of losing her again. Do you understand what I'm saying, Fulgor? Tell her father to go back and
keep working the mines. And out there . . . I imagine it wouldn't
be difficult to make the old man disappear in a place no one ever
visits. Don't you think?

—Could be.

—We need it to be. She needs to be an orphan. And it's our
duty to help those who've lost their families. Don't you agree?

—Doesn't seem too difficult.

—Then get going, Fulgor, get going.

—And if she finds out?

—Who's gonna tell her? Between the two of us, who's gonna
tell her?

—No one, I imagine.

—Forget "I imagine." Forget it right now and I'm sure everything's gonna turn out just fine. Remind him of all the work he
did to get La Andrómeda started. Send him back there so he can
keep at it. He can come and go as he pleases. But don't give him
any ideas about taking his daughter along. She'll stay here where
we can look after her. He'll get used to his work being out there
and his home here. Put it to him like that, Fulgor.

—Once again, I'm liking how you operate, patrón, as if you were getting your youthful energy back.

RAIN FALLS ON THE FIELDS in the valley surrounding Comala. A soft rain, strange for this region so accustomed to downpours. It's Sunday. The Indians have come down from Apango with their chamomile rosaries, their bunches of rosemary and thyme. They left behind their ocote pine since it's wet, as well as the oak mulch that's damp with all the rain. They display their herbs on the ground, under the arches of the portico, and then they wait.

The rain continues to fall, adding to the puddles.

The water forms rivers in the furrows where the corn has begun to grow. The men haven't come to market today, instead they're busy tearing down the corn rows so the water can find paths that won't wash away the young crop. They work in groups, out in the rain, navigating their way across flooded land, using shovels to break the soft mounds of earth, anchoring the young plants with their hands in hopes of protecting them so they might continue to grow.

The Indians wait. They feel it's not a good day. Perhaps that's why they shiver beneath straw cloaks drenched in the rain, not because they're cold, but because they're afraid. They gaze at the constant drizzle and then up at the sky that refuses to let go of the clouds.

No one shows up. The town feels empty. The woman asked them to bring her back some darning thread and a bit of sugar, and if possible, a sieve to make atole. As midday approaches, their wet cloaks weigh them down with moisture. They converse among themselves, telling jokes and laughing. Soaked in dew, the chamomile leaves glisten. They think: "None of this would matter, if only we'd brought a bit of pulque, but the hearts of the maguey plants have become a sea of water. So, it wasn't to be."

Hiding under her umbrella, Justina Díaz made her way down the road that came straight from the Media Luna, avoiding the streams of water that bubbled up onto the sidewalks. She made the sign of the cross as she passed in front of the entrance to the big church. She walked under the arches of the portico. The Indians turned to watch her. She felt their eyes on her as if she were being scrutinized. She stopped at the first seller, where she bought ten centavos' worth of rosemary before returning, followed by the stares of all those Indians lined up in rows.

«Things are so expensive these days —she said while heading back up the road toward the Media Luna—. This sad little bunch of rosemary for ten centavos. It's barely enough to give off any scent.»

The Indians packed up their displays once it began to get dark. They headed out into the rain, their wares weighing heavy on their backs. They stopped by the church to offer a prayer to the Virgin, leaving a handful of thyme as an offering. Then they set off for Apango, from where they had come. "Some other day," they said. As they walked, they told jokes, breaking out in laughter.

Justina Díaz entered Susana San Juan's bedroom and placed the rosemary on a shelf. The curtains were drawn, keeping the light out. And in that darkness, the only thing she could make out were shadows, forcing her to speculate. She supposed that Susana San Juan was asleep; she wished she were always so. Susana seemed to be sleeping and that made her happy, but then she heard a faint sigh as if coming from some corner of that unlit room.

—Justina! —something called to her.

She turned her head. There was no one there, but she felt a hand on her shoulder and breathing in her ears. A hushed voice:

«Leave this place, Justina. Gather your things and go. We no longer need you.»

—She needs me —she responded, standing up straight—. She's ill and she needs me.

—Not anymore, Justina. I'll stay and take care of her.

—Is that you, don Bartolomé? —but she didn't wait for an answer. She let out a shriek that dropped all the way down to the men and women returning from the fields, making them say: "That must be a human scream, but it sure doesn't sound as if it came from a human being."

The din of the rain muffles the noise and continues after other sounds dissipate. The falling drops turn to hail, weaving together the thread of life.

—What's wrong, Justina? Why'd you scream? —asked Susana San Juan.

—I didn't scream, Susana. You must've been dreaming.

—I told you I never dream. You don't think about me. I'm exhausted, all because you didn't put the cat out last night, and it wouldn't let me sleep.

—It slept with me, curled up between my legs. The poor thing was soaked so I let it stay in my bed, but it didn't make any noise.

—No, it didn't make noise. It just spent the night doing circus tricks, leaping back and forth from my feet to my head and meowing softly as if it were hungry.

—I fed it well, and it didn't leave my side all night. You're imagining things again, Susana.

—I'm telling you it startled me throughout the night with its constant jumping. Even though your cat is quite affectionate, I'd rather not have it around while I'm sleeping.

—You're seeing things, Susana. That's what it is. As soon as Pedro Páramo gets here, I'm going to tell him I can't stand you any longer. I'll tell him I'm leaving. There are plenty of good people who'll give me work. Not everyone's as fussy as you, nor are they gonna torment me the way you do. I'm out of here tomorrow, and I'll take the cat with me, so you won't get so upset anymore.

—You're not going anywhere, my wicked and loathsome Justina. You're not going anywhere because you won't find anyone who loves you the way I do.

—No, I'm not leaving, Susana. I won't leave. You know good and well I intend to look after you. Even if you make me regret it, I'll always take care of you.

She had looked after her since the day she was born. She had held her in her arms. She had taught her to walk, to take those first steps that to a child seem eternal. She had watched her mouth and eyes grow "like candies." "Mint candies are blue. Yellow and blue. Green and blue. With mint and spearmint inside." She nibbled at her legs. She amused her by letting her suckle at her breasts even though they had no milk so were nothing more than playthings. "Play with this —she would say—, play with these little toys of yours." She could have hugged her to pieces.

Outside, you could hear rain falling on banana leaves, while the drops that landed in the puddles made it sound as if the water were boiling.

The sheets were cold and damp. The drainpipes gurgled and foamed up, exhausted from working day and night and day. The water just kept flowing, pouring out in never-ending bubbles.

IT WAS MIDNIGHT and the rain falling outside drowned out all the other sounds.

Susana San Juan got up slowly. She gradually straightened her body and moved away from the bed. There it was again, a heaviness, at first down by her feet, but then rising along the edge of her body, searching for her face:

—Is that you, Bartolomé? —she asked.

She thought she heard the door creak, as if someone were coming or going. But there was only the rain, intermittent, cold, streaming down the banana leaves, boiling all on its own.

She fell back to sleep and didn't wake again until light illuminated the red bricks covered in dew in the gray dawn of a new day. She called out:

—Justina!

And she appeared immediately, as if she were already there, wrapping a blanket around her body.

—What is it, Susana?

—The cat. It was here again.

—My poor little Susana.

She laid her head on her breast and held her tight until Susana managed to lift that head and ask:

—Why are you crying? I'll tell Pedro Páramo you've been good to me. I won't say a thing about how your cat frightens me. Don't be like this, Justina.

—Your father's dead, Susana. He passed away two nights ago. People came by today to let us know there's nothing to be done, that he's already in the ground, that the journey was just too long for them to bring him here. You're all alone now, Susana.

—So, it was him —and she smiled—. You came to say goodbye —she said and smiled again.

MANY YEARS EARLIER, while she was still a child, he had told her:

—Climb down, Susana, and tell me what you see.

She was dangling from a rope that was pinching her waist and making her hands bleed, but she didn't want to let go since it seemed to be the only thread still connecting her to the outside world.

—I don't see anything, papá.

—Look carefully, Susana. Try to find something.

And he used his lamp to shine light on her.

—I don't see anything, papá.

—I'll lower you down a bit more. Let me know when you hit the bottom.

She had entered through a small opening between some boards, after walking along old decomposing planks that were splintered and covered in damp dirt:

—A bit lower, Susana, and you'll find what I'm talking about.

And she dropped down farther and farther, swinging in the void, her feet kicking at the air and finding no place to settle.

—Down farther, Susana, a bit farther. Tell me if you see anything.

When she felt ground beneath her, she stood still, too afraid to speak. The light of the lamp searched around her. A shout from above made her shudder:

—Hand me what's right there, Susana!

She picked the skull up in her hands, but let it drop as soon as the light hit it.

—It's a dead man's skull —she said.

—You should see something else right by it. Hand me everything you find.

The cadaver broke into pieces. The jawbone came off as if it were made of sugar. She slowly handed each bit of the skeleton up to him until she got to the feet and then passed him one toe joint at a time. But the skull had been first, and that round object had crumbled in her hands.

—Look for something more, Susana. Money. Round disks of gold. Look for those, Susana.

She lost all sense of herself, coming to many days later in the cold, in the frigid gaze of her father's eyes.

That's why she was laughing now.

—I knew it was you, Bartolomé.

And poor Justina, sobbing on Susana's bosom, right over her heart, raised up when she noticed she was laughing and that her laughter was becoming uncontrollable.

Outside it continued to rain. The Indians had left. It was Monday, and the valley surrounding Comala was still drowning in rain.

THE WIND BLEW NONSTOP in those days. The same wind that had brought the rain. The rain had stopped, but the gusts remained. Out in the milpa the plants aired out their leaves and bent down into the furrows to find shelter. During the day, the wind was tolerable, twisting the ivy and rattling the roof tiles, but at night it moaned and moaned without end. Pavilions of clouds passed silently through the sky, so low it seemed as if they were strolling across the earth.

Susana San Juan listens as the wind slaps against the closed window. She lies in bed with her arms behind her head, contemplating, listening to the sounds of the night, listening as the night is dragged here and there by the restless blowing of the wind. Then, abruptly, everything stops.

Someone has opened the door. A wind gust blows out the lamp. She sees the darkness, and her thoughts cease. She makes out a faint rustling. Suddenly she hears the uneven palpitations of her heart. Through her closed eyelids she notices the flame of a candle.

She doesn't open her eyes. Her hair pours across her face. The light flashes on drops of sweat on her lips. She asks:

—Is that you, Father?

—Yes, my child, I am your Father.

She peers through half-opened eyes. The hair draped across her face seems to mingle with a shadow on the ceiling, its head located right above her face. The blurred figure of its body stands in front of her, just beyond the drizzle of her eyelashes. A dim light, a light where the heart should be, in the shape of a tiny heart throbbing like a flickering flame. "Your heart is dying of sorrow —she thought to herself—. I know you've come to tell me Florencio is dead, but I already know that. Don't concern yourself with others, don't worry about me. My pain is tucked away somewhere safe. Don't let your heart be snuffed out."

She forced her body out of bed and dragged it over to where Father Rentería was standing.

—Let me console you with my grief! —she said, protecting the flame with her hands.

Father Rentería let her approach, and he looked on as she encircled the burning candle with her hands and then touched her face to the flame. The smell of burning flesh compelled him to pull the candle away and to blow it out with a quick breath.

As darkness returned, she ran to find refuge beneath her sheets.

Father Rentería told her:

—I've come to comfort you, my child.

—Then you may leave, Father —she responded—. And don't come back. I don't need you.

She listened as the footsteps receded, something that always left her with a sense of cold, of trembling, and of fear.

—Why do you come to visit if you're already dead?

Father Rentería closed the door and stepped into the night air. The wind continued to blow.

A MAN THEY CALLED El Tartamudo showed up at the Media Luna asking for Pedro Páramo.

—Why do you want to see him?

—I need to t-talk with him.

—He's not here.

—When he gets b-back t-tell him it's about d-don Fulgor.

—I'll look for him, but it may take a few hours.

—T-tell him it's ur-urgent.

—I'll tell him.

The man they called El Tartamudo waited on his horse. After a while, Pedro Páramo, whom he'd never seen, stood in front of him:

—How can I help you?

—I need to t-talk d-directly with the p-patrón.

—You're talking to him. What do you want?

—Well, j-just this. They've k-killed don Fulgor S-Sedano. I was w-with him. We were on the r-road to the s-spillways to figure out why the water had d-dried up. While d-doing that a b-bunch of men c-came over. Out of the c-crowd a voice spoke up and said: "I know h-him. He's the foreman over at the M-Media Luna."

»Th-they didn't p-pay me no mind. B-but they t-told don Fulgor to let g-go of his horse. Said they were r-revolutionaries. Th-that they w-wanted your lands. "R-run! —they told don Fulgor—. Go t-tell your patrón we'll be s-seeing him later!" He took off, t-terrified. Not t-too fast c-cause of how heavy he was, b-but he ran. They k-killed him as he ran. He d-died with one f-foot in the air, the other on the g-ground.

»I didn't m-move. I w-waited for n-night, and now here I am t-telling you what h-happened.«

—What are you waiting for? Get going. Go let those men know I'm here if they need anything. Tell them I'm the one they'll have to deal with. But first, swing by La Consagración. You know who El Tilcuate is, right? He'll be there. Tell him I need to see him. And tell those other men I'll expect a visit as soon as they're available. What sort of revolutionaries are they?

—D-don't know. That's j-just what they c-called themselves.

—Tell El Tilcuate I need him here immediately.

—Sure thing, p-patrón.

Pedro Páramo shut himself back up in his office. He felt old and overwhelmed. He wasn't concerned about Fulgor, who by then already "belonged more to the next world than to this one." He had given all he could and, although still useful, he was no longer more so than anyone else. "Besides, those fools have no idea how much El Tilcuate's gonna make them suffer," he mused.

He thought again about Susana San Juan, always hidden away in her room, sleeping, and when she wasn't, acting as if she were. He had spent the previous night leaning against the wall, watching her through the dim light as she fidgeted in her bed, her face bathed in sweat, her hands pulling at the sheets and squeezing the pillow before falling unconscious.

Each of the nights he had spent by her side since bringing her here to live had been like this one, full of pain and unending restlessness. He wondered when it would end.

Someday soon, he hoped. Nothing lasts forever. There's not a single memory, no matter how intense, that won't fade eventually.

If only he knew what was causing her affliction, what was making her thrash about in her sleep as if she were being ripped to shreds and left broken.

He thought he knew her. But even if that were not the case, was it not enough to know that she was the creature he most loved in all the world? Beyond that, and this was what mattered most, it would allow him to leave this life illuminated by this image that would erase all other memories.

But to what world did Susana San Juan belong? That was one thing that Pedro Páramo was never able to figure out.

«THE WARMTH OF THE SAND felt good against my body. My eyes were closed, my arms outstretched, my legs open to the sea breeze. And the sea before me, distant, the rising tide leaving traces of foam on my feet . . .»

—That's her speaking again, Juan Preciado. Don't forget to tell me what she says.

«. . . It was early in the morning. The sea rushed in and out in waves, the green water releasing its foam before withdrawing, cleansed, in hushed ripples.

»—The only way I like to swim in the sea is naked —I told him. And that first day he followed me in, undressed as well, looking phosphorescent as he emerged from the water. There weren't any seagulls, only those birds they call "ugly beaks," the ones that growl as if they were snoring and then disappear when the sun comes out. He followed me that first day and felt all alone, even though I was with him.

»—It's as if you were one of those birds —he told me—, just one among many. I prefer you at night, when we're both lying on the same pillow, in the dark and between the sheets.

»And he left.

»I came back. I would always come back. The sea soaks my ankles and then recedes, it soaks my knees, then my thighs; it wraps its tender arm around my waist and caresses my breasts; it embraces my neck and presses against my shoulders. I immerse myself in the sea, fully. I give myself over to its steady force, its gentle possession, holding nothing back.

»—I like to bathe in the sea —I told him.

»But he doesn't understand.

»And the following day, I returned to the sea, to purify myself. To give myself over to its waves.»

THE MEN APPEARED just as the afternoon sky was turning to dusk. They were armed with carbines, with cartridge belts across their chests. There were about twenty of them. Pedro Páramo

invited them to dinner. They sat around the table in silence and
without removing their sombreros. The only noise they made
came as they drank their chocolate and chewed down one tortilla
after another together with the beans they were served.

Pedro Páramo looked on. None of the faces seemed familiar.
El Tilcuate stood behind him, waiting in the shadows.

—Señores —he called out when he saw they had finished
eating—, what else can I do for you?

—This all belongs to you? —one of them asked while waving
his hand.

But he was interrupted by another:

—I'll do the talking here!

—Fine. What can I do for you? —Pedro Páramo asked again.

—As you can see, we've taken up arms.

—And?

—And that's all. You think it's nothing?

—For what reason exactly?

—Because others have done the same thing. Or haven't you
heard? Just wait a bit, till we get instructions, then we'll let you
know what our cause is. Until then, we'll hang out here.

—I know what our cause is —said another—. And if you
want, I'll explain it to you. We've rebelled against the government
and against your kind because we're tired of putting up with you.
Against the government for being corrupt and against you all
for being a filthy bunch of freeloaders and thieves. And I'm not
gonna say anything more about our esteemed government since
what we've got to say to them, we'll say at the point of a gun.

—How much do you need for your revolution? —Pedro
Páramo asked—. Perhaps I could help.

—The gentleman here makes some sense, Perseverancio.
Perhaps you should hold your tongue. It might be good to have a
rich friend who could help us out, and who better than this señor
right here? What do you think, Casildo, how much could we use?

—Maybe he should hand over whatever he feels is best, out of the goodness of his heart.

—This guy wouldn't give water to a man dying of thirst. I say we make the most of being here now and pilfer everything he's got, right down to the tortillas he shoved down his dirty little gullet.

—Settle down, Perseverancio. Honey catches more flies than vinegar. Maybe we can come to an agreement. What do you say, Casildo?

—Well, thinking on it, I'd say twenty thousand pesos would be a good start. What do the rest of you think? Or maybe the señor considers that small change seeing how he's so excited to lend a hand. So why don't we say fifty thousand. How does that sound?

—I'll give you a hundred thousand pesos —Pedro Páramo said—. How many of you are there?

—About three hundred.

—Well then. I'm gonna give you another three hundred men to strengthen your contingent. You'll have both the men and the money within the week. The money's a gift, the men are on loan. Send them back this way when you're done with them. Do we have a deal?

—I don't see why not.

—Then we'll see you in a week, señores. It's been a pleasure.

—Okay then —said the last one to leave—. Just know if you don't come through, you'll be hearing from Perseverancio, and that's me.

Pedro Páramo saw him off with a handshake.

—WHO DO YOU FIGURE was the one in charge? —he later asked El Tilcuate.

—Well, I'd say it's the one with the big gut who sat right in the middle and never once looked up. I'd bet it's him . . . I'm seldom wrong, don Pedro.

—No, Damasio, you're the one in charge. Or you gonna tell me you're not itching to join the revolt?

—I'm more than ready. Considering how much I like a good fight.

—You just saw how this all works, so you don't need any advice from me. Gather three hundred men you can trust and join up with those rebels. Tell them you've got the men I promised. You'll figure out the rest on your own.

—What do I tell them about the money? Do I hand that over to them as well?

—I'm gonna give you ten pesos for each man. Enough for their immediate expenses. Tell them I'm keeping the rest safe here and at their disposal. It wouldn't be wise to haul so much money around. By the way, how'd you like to own that little ranch out at Puerta de Piedra? It's yours as of now. Take a message to Gerardo Trujillo, the lawyer over in Comala, and he'll put your name on the deed. What do you think of that, Damasio?

—Goes without saying, patrón. Although with or without the ranch, I'd join in just for the fun of it. As if you didn't already know that. I appreciate it all the same. At least this way my old lady will have something to keep her busy while I'm out running wild.

—And while you're at it, take a few cows with you. That ranch needs to be stirred up a bit.

—Would you mind if I took some of the Brahmans?

—Take whatever you want, and whatever you think your wife can take care of. Now getting back to our business, make sure you don't wander too far from my property so when others show up, they'll see the land is already occupied. And come see me when you can or when you've got news.

—See you soon, patrón.

—**WHAT'S SHE SAYING**, Juan Preciado?

—She says she used to bury her feet between his legs. Feet that were cold as stones, which his legs would warm like loaves of bread baking in an oven. She says he would nibble at her feet saying they were like freshly baked golden loaves. And that she would sleep curled up next to him, pressing herself into his very being, lost in nothingness as she felt the flesh of her body yield, opening like a furrow that gives way to a plow that burns at first, before turning tepid, and then feels sweet, striking against her soft flesh, sinking a bit, and then some more until she would cry out. And yet his death had been more painful still. That's what she's saying.

—Who's she talking about?

—Someone who died before her, I'm sure.

—But who could that be?

—I don't know. She says that the night he was slow getting home she was sure he'd come in late, perhaps before dawn. She barely noticed a thing, just that her feet, which had been lonely and cold, then seemed to be covered, as if someone had tried to keep them warm. After a bit, when she woke, her feet were wrapped in the newspaper she'd been reading while waiting for him, which had fallen to the ground when she could no longer stay awake. She says her feet were still tucked in that newspaper when they came to tell her he was dead.

—The box she's buried in must have just split open because I hear something that sounds like boards cracking.

—Yes, I hear it too.

THAT NIGHT HER DREAMS RETURNED. Why such intense memories of all those things? Why not simply death, without the heartfelt melodies of the past?

—Florencio is dead, señora.

How big that man was! So tall! And his voice was harsh. Dry as the driest dirt. And his shape was out of focus, or was it only later that he started to seem blurred? As if rain were falling between the two of them. "What was it he said? Something about Florencio? Which Florencio was he talking about? Mine? Oh! But why hadn't I cried and drowned myself in tears to wash away my grief? Lord, Thou dost not exist! I asked Thee to protect him. To look after him. That's all I asked for. But all Thou carest for is the soul. And what I want from him is his body. Naked and warmed by love, simmering with desire, massaging the trembling of my arms and breasts. My transparent body suspended by his. My slender frame supported by and lost in his strength. What am I to do with my lips now when I don't have his mouth to occupy them? What am I to do with my aching lips?"

As Susana San Juan tossed uneasily, Pedro Páramo was on his feet, standing by the door, watching and counting the seconds of this new dream that seemed to drag on. The oil of the lamp crackled as the flame slowly weakened. Soon it would go out.

If only it were a physical ailment that tormented her, rather than these restless dreams, these unrelenting and exhausting hallucinations, then he could seek out some sort of relief. That's what Pedro Páramo imagined as he gazed at Susana San Juan, attentive to her every movement. What would happen if her life were to be snuffed out along with the light of the delicate flame that allowed him to watch over her?

Later, as he left, he closed the door without making a sound. Outside, the fresh night air erased her image from Pedro Páramo's mind.

Susana San Juan awoke a few moments before dawn. Drenched in sweat. She threw the heavy blankets to the ground and refused even the warmth of the sheets. She lay there naked, cooled by the morning breeze. She sighed and then fell back to sleep.

That's how Father Rentería found her hours later, naked and asleep.

—**HAVE YOU HEARD**, don Pedro, that El Tilcuate was defeated?

—I know there was a gun battle last night since I heard the commotion, but I don't know anything more. Who told you that, Gerardo?

—A few of the injured showed up in Comala. My wife helped bandage them up. Said they were with Damasio and that many of them had died. Seems they ran into a group calling themselves Villistas.

—Good Lord, Gerardo! Seems bad days are headed our way. What are you going to do?

—I'm leaving, don Pedro. Headed to Sayula. I'll set up there and start over.

—You lawyers have that advantage; you can move your operation anywhere, as long as no one busts you in the jaw.

—Don't believe it, don Pedro. We lawyers always have our problems. Besides, it hurts to cut ties with clients like you, and your consideration will be missed. But we always end up tearing our world apart, if you don't mind me saying so. Where would you like me to leave your papers?

—Don't leave them. Take them with you. Or won't you be able to keep looking after my affairs where you're going?

—I appreciate your confidence, don Pedro. With all sincerity. Although I must insist that it would be impossible for me to continue. Certain irregularities . . . Let's say . . . A few items that only you should know about. Ones that could be used against you if they were to fall into the wrong hands. It'd be safer if they were to stay with you.

—You're right, Gerardo. Leave them here. I'll burn them. With or without papers, who's going to challenge my right to the land?

—I'm sure no one will, don Pedro. No one. Now, if you'll excuse me.

—Go with God, Gerardo.

—What did you say?

—I said, may God be with you.

The lawyer Gerardo Trujillo left without hurrying. He was already old, but not so old that he needed to leave at such a slow pace, so reluctantly. The truth is, he expected a reward. He had served don Lucas, may he rest in peace, father of don Pedro, followed by don Pedro, and then Miguel after that, son of don Pedro. The truth is, he expected compensation. A significant and valuable payment. He had said as much to his wife:

—I'm going to say goodbye to don Pedro. I know he'll want to give me a bonus. And I'm sure we'll be able to use that money to set ourselves up well in Sayula and live comfortably the rest of our lives.

But why do women always have doubts? Do they get their instincts from on high or something? She wasn't sure he would get anything:

—You'll have to break your back in Sayula to get ahead since you're not gonna get anything out of this place.

—Why do you say that?

—I just know.

He kept walking slowly toward the door, listening for someone to call out: "Hey, Gerardo! I'm so distracted I didn't think things through. But I'm indebted to you for favors that can't be repaid with cash. Take this: a small gift."

But the call never came. He passed through the door and unfastened the halter he had used to secure his horse to the hitching post. He climbed into the saddle and headed in the direction of Comala, trying not to get so far away he wouldn't be able to hear if someone called after him. When he realized the Media Luna was fading in the distance, he thought: "It would be too degrading to ask him for a loan."

—I'M BACK, DON PEDRO, because I don't feel right about how I left things. I'd be happy to continue looking after your affairs.

He spoke while seated once again in Pedro Páramo's office, in the same spot he had been less than a half hour earlier.

—That's fine, Gerardo. The papers are there, right where you left them.

—I'd also appreciate . . . Certain expenses . . . Moving costs . . . A modest advance on my fees . . . And a bit extra if you feel it's warranted.

—Five hundred?

—Couldn't we say a little, just a little more?

—Would you be happy with a thousand?

—Or what about five?

—Five what? Five thousand pesos? I don't have that. You know quite well that everything's invested. In land, animals. You know that. Take a thousand. I can't imagine you'll need more than that.

He contemplated for a moment. His head hung low. He heard coins jingling on the desk where Pedro Páramo was counting them out. He remembered don Lucas, who always put off paying his fees. And don Pedro, who had wiped the slate clean. And his son, Miguel: what a nuisance that boy had been!

He had gotten Miguel out of jail at least fifteen times, if not more. And then that time he murdered that man, what was his name? Rentería, that's it. His name was Rentería, and they had placed a pistol in his dead hand. That gave Miguelito quite the scare, although he later laughed about it. That alone, how much would it have cost don Pedro if things had gone further, and the law had become involved? And what about all those sexual assaults? All the times he was forced to pay out of his own pocket to keep those women quiet: "Be grateful you're gonna have a light-skinned child!" he would say.

—Here it is, Gerardo. Spend it wisely since when it's gone, it's gone.

And Gerardo, still deep in thought, responded:

—You're right, and when the dead are gone, they're gone. —And then he added—: Unfortunately.

FIRST LIGHT WAS STILL a long way off. The sky was filled with stars, fat ones, swollen by the long night. The moon had come out for a short while, before disappearing again. It was one of those sorrowful moons that no one gazes at, no one notices. It had hung there for a time, disfigured, giving off no light, before rushing to hide behind the hills.

Off in the distance and lost in the darkness came the bellowing of bulls.

«Those animals never sleep —said Damiana Cisneros—. They never sleep. They're like the Devil, always searching for souls he can drag down to Hell.»

She rolled over in bed, moving her face next to the wall. That's when she heard the knocking.

She held her breath and opened her eyes. Once again, she heard three hard knocks, as if someone were rapping their knuckles against the wall. Not here beside her, farther away but on the same wall.

«Good Lord! That's got to be San Pascual Bailón knocking three times as a sign to one of his followers that the hour of their death has arrived.»

She wasn't really worried the knocking was for her, since her rheumatism had kept her from making a novena in his honor in such a long while. And although she was a bit startled, that was perhaps more out of curiosity than fear.

She got up quietly from her bed and peered out the window. The fields were dark. Even so, she knew the terrain so well she was able to spot Pedro Páramo as he swung his large body up and through the window that belonged to young Margarita.

—Ah, that don Pedro! —Damiana said—. He just can't stop chasing women. What I don't understand is why he likes to do everything in secret. If he'd let me know, I could have told Margarita the patrón needed her tonight, and he wouldn't even have had to get out of bed.

She closed the window when she heard the bulls bellowing. She threw herself on her bed, pulling the blanket up to her ears, and then she began thinking about what must be happening to young Margarita.

A bit later, she had to remove her nightgown since the night had begun to grow hot . . .

—Damiana! —she heard.

And she was a young woman again.

—Open the door, Damiana!

Her heart was beating as if a toad were trapped in her ribcage.

—What for, patrón?

—Open up, Damiana!

—But I'm already asleep, patrón.

Then she heard don Pedro disappear down the corridor, stomping his feet, as he tended to do when irritated.

To make it easier on him and avoid his anger, the following night she left the door ajar and climbed into bed naked.

But Pedro Páramo never returned.

That's why now, as an old woman, having earned the respect and now in charge of all the servants working at the Media Luna, she still thought of that night long ago when the patrón called to her:

«Open the door, Damiana!»

And she lay back down imagining how happy young Margarita must be just now.

Later she heard more knocking, but this time at the main door, as if someone were beating it with the butt of a rifle.

She opened her window again and peered back into the night. She couldn't see a thing, although it seemed to her that the land was simmering, just as it does after a heavy rain fills the ground with worms. She sensed that something was rising, something like the heat of scores of men. She heard frogs croaking, crickets, the stillness of night during the rainy season. Then once again she heard rifle butts banging against the door.

A lantern splashed its light across the faces of a group of men. Then it went out.

«Whatever this is, it doesn't concern me,» Damiana Cisneros said, and then she closed the window.

—I HEARD YOU were defeated, Damasio. How'd you let that happen?

—You're misinformed, patrón. Nothing's happened to me. I still have all my men. There are seven hundred of us, as well as a few tagalongs. It's just that some of the older guys got tired of sitting around and started taking potshots at a band of pelones that turned out to be a whole army. Villa's men, wouldn't you know?

—Where'd they come from?

—From up north, and they've been running roughshod over everything they come up against. They seem to be bouncing around getting a feel for the land. They're powerful. Can't deny that.

—So why haven't you joined up with them? I've already said you need to stick with whoever's winning.

—I'm already with them.

—Then why are you here to see me?

—We need cash, patrón. We're tired of eating nothing but meat. Can't stand the taste of it no more. And nobody'll give us anything on credit. That's why we've shown up here, to see if you can help us out so we won't have to pilfer from others. If we were out and about, it wouldn't bother us to "pay a visit" to the neighbors, but around here we're all related, and we'd feel bad just taking stuff. In short, we need a bit of money to buy a few things, even if it's just a few tortillas with some chilies. We're tired of eating nothing but meat.

—You gonna start being difficult now, Damasio?

—Not at all, patrón. I'm just asking on behalf of my boys. Personally, I don't need a thing.

—It's good you're looking out for your men, but you should lean on other people to get what you want. I've already given, so make do with that. I'm certainly not gonna tell you what to do, but hasn't it occurred to you to go after Contla? Or why else are you in the revolution? You've got it all wrong if you're out asking for charity. Might as well go back to your wife and raise hens. Go strike at some town! If you're the one running around risking your neck, why the hell shouldn't others be asked to give something to the cause? Contla is overflowing with rich folk. Take a bit of what they have. Or do you imagine you're their wet nurse, with their interests at heart? No, Damasio. Make them understand you're not having fun, not playing around. Hit them hard and you'll knock some centavos loose.

—Whatever you say, patrón. I always learn something of value from you.

—Make good use of it, then.

Pedro Páramo looked on as the men headed out. He sensed
the dark horses as they trotted in front of him, merging into the
night. The sweat and the dust, the shaking of the earth. When
once again he was able to see the glow of fireflies, he knew that
everyone was gone. He was the only one left, stiff as the trunk
of a tree that is beginning to rot on the inside.

He thought of Susana San Juan. He thought of the girl he
had slept with just moments earlier. Her small, frightened body
trembling so hard it seemed her heart would burst from her
chest. "Sweet little thing," he said to her. And he had held her
tight, hoping her flesh might transform into that of Susana San
Juan. "A woman who was not of this world."

AS THE MORNING LIGHT BREAKS, the day reluctantly
begins revealing itself. One can almost hear the earth rotating
on rusted hinges, the trembling of an ancient world pouring out
its darkness.

—Is it true that the night is full of sin, Justina?

—Yes, Susana.

—For certain it's true?

—It must be, Susana.

—And what do you think life is, Justina, if not sin? Do you
hear it? Do you hear how the earth creaks?

—No, Susana, I don't hear a thing. My destiny is not as grand
as yours.

—You'd be amazed. Amazed, I'm telling you, if you could
hear what I'm hearing.

Justina kept cleaning the room. She ran the rag several times
over the wet floorboards. She cleaned up the water from the
shattered vase. She picked up the flowers. She placed the glass
shards in the bucket of water.

—How many birds have you killed in your life, Justina?

—Many, Susana.

—And it didn't make you feel sad?

—It did, Susana.

—So, what are you waiting for to die?

—For death, Susana.

—If that's all you're waiting for, it'll come. Don't you worry.

Susana San Juan was sitting up against her pillows. Her eyes uneasy, peering off in all directions. Her hands on her belly, clasped together as if they were a protective shell. There was a soft buzzing sound like wings that passed above her head. And the noise of the pulley from the well. The sounds people make as they awaken.

—Do you believe in Hell, Justina?

—Yes, Susana. And in Heaven as well.

—I only believe in Hell —she said. And she closed her eyes.

Susana San Juan was sleeping again when Justina left the room. Outside, the sun was crackling. Along the way, she ran into Pedro Páramo.

—How's the señora?

—Bad —she responded, dropping her head.

—Is she complaining?

—No, señor, she doesn't complain about a thing. But, as they say, the dead no longer make a fuss. The señora is lost to us all.

—Hasn't Father Rentería come to see her?

—He came by last night and heard her confession. She should've taken Communion today, but maybe she's not in a state of grace since Father Rentería hasn't brought it. He said he'd come by early but, as you can see, the sun's up and he's not here. She must not be in a state of grace.

—In whose grace?

—In God's grace, señor.

—Don't be silly, Justina.

—Whatever you say, señor.

Pedro Páramo opened the door and stood next to it, allowing a shaft of light to fall upon Susana San Juan. He noticed her eyes closed tight, like someone feeling an inner pain, her mouth moist and slightly open, and the bedsheets being pulled down by unaware hands, revealing a naked body beginning to shudder.

He crossed the short distance separating him from the bed and covered her nakedness as her body continued thrashing about like a worm whose convulsions grow more and more violent. He leaned toward her ear and said: "Susana!" And then again: "Susana!"

The door opened and Father Rentería entered without making a sound, until he said softly:

—I'm here to give you Communion, my child.

He waited for Pedro Páramo to lift her and sit her up against the headboard. Susana San Juan, still half asleep, extended her tongue and swallowed the Host. Then she said: "We've had a great time, Florencio," before burying herself once again in the tomb of her sheets.

—YOU SEE THAT WINDOW over at the Media Luna, doña Fausta, where there's always been a light?

—No, Ángeles. I don't see any window.

—That's because it went dark just now. You think something bad might've happened out at the Media Luna? For three years now that window's been lit up, night after night. People who've been there say the room belongs to Pedro Páramo's wife, a poor little thing who's out of her mind and afraid of the dark. And look at it now: the light's gone out. Could it mean something bad?

—Maybe she's died. She was quite sick. They say she no longer recognized people, and that she talked to herself. What a punishment Pedro Páramo must have endured being married to that woman.

—That poor man don Pedro.

—No, Fausta. He deserves it. That and more.

—Look, the window's still dark.

—Stop worrying about that window and let's get to bed. It's much too late for two old women like us to be wandering the streets.

And the women, who had left the church at about eleven at night, disappeared under the arches of the portico as they watched the shadow of a man crossing the plaza in the direction of the Media Luna.

—Hey, doña Fausta, you think that man over there is Doctor Valencia?

—It seems to be him, although I'm so blind I don't know if I'd be able to recognize him.

—Remember how he always wears white pants and a dark jacket? I'd bet something bad is going on out at the Media Luna. Look how fast he's moving, as if something were hurrying him along.

—He wouldn't move like that if it weren't serious. I'm tempted to go back and tell Father Rentería to head out there. Wouldn't want that poor creature to die without confessing.

—Don't even think it, Ángeles. Heaven forbid. After everything she's suffered, who'd want her to leave this life without last rites and end up tormented in the next? Then again, the mystics will tell you the insane have no need to confess, that they're innocent even if their souls are impure. Only God knows . . . Now look! You can see the light in that window again. Hopefully everything turns out okay. If someone in that house dies just imagine what'll happen to all the work we've put in the past several days getting the church ready for the Nativity. Given how important don Pedro is, our celebration would be called off in a heartbeat.

—You always imagine the worst, doña Fausta. You should do what I do and leave it in the hands of Divine Providence. Say an Ave María to the Virgin and I'm sure nothing bad will happen between now and tomorrow morning. Beyond that, let the Lord's will be done. After all, she can't be very happy in this life.

—You know, Ángeles, you always lift my spirits. Your words will comfort me as I head to bed, and they say the thoughts you have while sleeping go straight to Heaven. I hope mine can rise that far. See you tomorrow.

—See you tomorrow, Fausta.

The two old women slipped into their homes through doors they opened only partway. As silence returned, the night closed back in on the town.

—**MY MOUTH IS FILLED** with dirt.

—Yes, Father.

—Don't say: "Yes, Father." Repeat what I say.

—What are you gonna say? You'll hear my confession again? Why?

—This won't be a confession, Susana. I've just come to talk with you. To prepare you for death.

—Am I going to die?

—Yes, child.

—Then why don't you leave me in peace? I want to rest. Someone must have asked you to come chase away my dreams. To stay with me till I no longer feel drowsy. But then what'll I do to find sleep again? Nothing, Father. Why don't you just leave me be and let me rest?

—I'll leave you in peace, Susana. As you repeat the words I say, you'll slowly doze off. You'll feel as if you were lulling yourself to sleep. And after you drift away no one will wake you . . . You'll never wake again.

—That's good, Father. I'll do as you ask.

Father Rentería, sitting on the edge of the bed, his hands on Susana San Juan's shoulders, his mouth nearly touching her ear to avoid having to speak loudly, carefully whispered each of his words: "My mouth is filled with dirt." But then he paused. He tried to notice whether her lips were moving. And he saw them tremble, although without emitting a sound.

«My mouth is filled with you, with your mouth. Your tight, full lips as if they were pressing against and biting mine . . .»

She paused as well. She glanced at Father Rentería and saw him distant, as if he were behind a window that has clouded over.

Then she heard his voice as it once again warmed the inside of her ear:

—I swallow saliva that foams in my mouth. I chew on clods of dirt crawling with worms that bunch together in my throat and scrape the roof of my mouth . . . My mouth caves in, twisting out of shape, pierced by teeth that bore down into it, devouring it. My nose turns to mush. The fluid in my eyes seeps out. The hair on my head burns in a sudden blaze . . .

He was surprised at how calm Susana San Juan had remained. He wished he could divine her thoughts and watch her heart as it worked to resist the images he was planting in her mind. He looked into her eyes, and she met his gaze. And he imagined seeing her lips trying to force a smile.

—There's more. The sight of God. The gentle light of His infinite Heaven. The jubilation of the cherubim and the song of the seraphim. The happiness in God's eyes, the last fleeting image seen by those condemned to eternal suffering. On top of that, an endless torment added to our earthly sorrow. The marrow of our bones turned to hot ash and the veins that carry our blood to strings of fire, forcing us to wallow in an immense pain that never subsides and is stoked by the wrath of God.

«He sheltered me in his arms. He gave me love.»

Father Rentería glanced at the others who were there await-
ing the final moment. Standing near the door was Pedro Páramo,
his arms crossed, followed by Doctor Valencia and a few other
men. Farther back, in the shadows, a handful of women waited
impatiently to begin the prayer for the dead.

He would have liked to stand up. To anoint the invalid with
the holy oils and declare: "I have finished." But no, he wasn't
yet finished. He couldn't administer the sacrament to a woman
without knowing the state of her repentance.

He was filled with doubt. Perhaps there was nothing for
which she needed to repent, nothing for which he needed to
absolve her. He leaned over her again and, shaking her by the
shoulders, said in a soft voice:

—You're about to enter the presence of God. And severe is
His judgment of sinners.

Then, as he tried once more to whisper in her ear, she shook
her head:

—Go now, Father! Don't torment yourself over me. I'm at
peace, and I want to sleep.

One of the women hiding in the shadows could be heard
weeping.

With that, Susana San Juan seemed to spring back to life. She
sat up in bed and said:

—Justina, do me the favor of finding some other place to cry!

Then she felt as if her head had dropped onto her abdomen. She
tried to lift it back up, to separate it from her belly, which pressed
against her eyes and made it difficult to breathe, but with each effort
she tumbled farther, as if she were sinking into the night.

—**I WAS THERE**. I saw doña Susanita die.

—What did you say, Dorotea?

—I said what I just said.

AT DAWN, EVERYONE was awakened by the tolling of bells. It was the morning of the eighth of December. A gray morning. Not cold, but gray. The ringing began with the largest bell. The others joined in. Some imagined it was a call to High Mass and doors began to open, just a few, those that belonged to those early risers who waited restlessly for the first bells to announce the end of the night. But the tolling lasted longer than it should have. And it was no longer coming just from the bells of the main church, but also from those of the Sangre de Cristo, the Cruz Verde, and perhaps those of the Santuario. By noon the ringing had not yet ceased. Then night came. Day and night the bells kept sounding in unison, growing louder and louder until the noise became a deafening lament. Everyone shouted to be able to hear each other. "What's going on?" they asked.

By the third day the whole town was deaf. It was impossible to speak with the clanging that hung in the air. But the bells kept ringing and ringing, some of them now cracked and producing a hollow sound like a jug.

—Doña Susana's dead.

—Dead? Who?

—The señora.

—Yours?

—Pedro Páramo's.

People began showing up from all over, drawn in by the constant ringing. They came from Contla as if on a pilgrimage. And from even farther away. Who knows where it came from, but there was even a circus with a merry-go-round and flying chairs. And musicians. At first they came to gawk, but soon enough they made themselves at home and started playing serenades. Little by little, everything turned into a big party. Comala was teeming with people, with celebrations, and with loud noises, just like during feast days, when moving around town is always so difficult.

The bells finally stopped ringing, but the party continued. There was no way to make people understand that this was a question of mourning, that these were days of grief. Nor was there any way to get them to leave. Instead, more people kept coming.

The Media Luna stood alone, in silence, everyone walking around barefoot and speaking in hushed voices. They buried Susana San Juan and few in Comala noticed. They were celebrating. There were cockfights and music, and shouting from drunkards and people playing games of chance. The lights from town reached all the way out here and appeared as a halo above the gray sky. Those were gray days, sad ones for the Media Luna. Don Pedro didn't say a word. He didn't leave his room. He vowed to take revenge on Comala:

—I'll cross my arms and Comala will die of hunger.

And that's what he did.

EL TILCUATE KEPT COMING BACK:

—We're with Carranza now.

—Good.

—Now we're with General Obregón.

—Good.

—They've made peace. We're on our own.

—Wait awhile. Don't disband your men. This can't last long.

—Father Rentería has taken up arms. Should we be with him or against him?

—No question about it. Take the side of the government.

—But we're irregulars. They consider us insurgents.

—Then go ahead and rest.

—When I'm still itching to fight?

—Then do what you want.

—I'll join up with the priest. I like how they yell. Besides, fighting on his side your salvation is guaranteed.

—Do whatever you want.

PEDRO PÁRAMO WAS SITTING in an old equipal chair beside the main door to the Media Luna moments before the last shadow of night disappeared. He was alone, and had been for perhaps the last three hours. He couldn't sleep. He had forgotten what sleep was, forgotten the very passage of time: "We old folks don't sleep much, almost never. We doze off every now and then, but we never stop thinking. It's the only thing I have left to do." Then he added out loud: "It won't be long now. Not long at all."

And he continued: «It's been a long time since you left, Susana. The light was the same then as it is now; not quite as red, but it was the same miserable, lifeless light draped in a white tissue of mist. It was the same time of day. And I was sitting right here, next to this doorway, seeing the sun rise, watching as you went away along the path toward Heaven; over there, where the sky was beginning to unfurl its lights, you faded slowly into the shadows of the earth, leaving me behind.

»That was the last time I saw you. Your body brushed against the branches of the paradise tree that stands beside the path, its last leaves following in your wake. Then you were gone. I cried out: "Come back, Susana!"»

Pedro Páramo continued moving his lips, whispering words. Then he closed his mouth and opened his eyes just enough for them to reflect the vague light of dawn.

The morning was breaking.

AT THAT SAME HOUR, Gamaliel Villalpando's mother, doña Inés, was sweeping the street in front of her son's store when

Abundio Martínez arrived and entered through the half-open door. He found Gamaliel asleep on the counter with his sombrero over his face to keep the flies away. He waited there quite a while for him to wake up. He was still waiting when doña Inés finished her sweeping, poked her son in the ribs with the end of her broom, and said to him:

—You've got a customer. Get up!

Annoyed and grumbling, Gamaliel got up. His eyes were bloodshot from having stayed up too late and from serving a bunch of drunkards, getting smashed right alongside them. As he sat on the counter, he cursed his mother, he cursed himself, and he repeatedly cursed his life that "wasn't worth a damn." Then he lay back down with his hands between his legs, mumbling obscenities as he fell back to sleep:

—It's not my fault if drunks are still out this time of day.

—My poor boy. Forgive him, Abundio. Poor guy spent the night looking after a group of out-of-towners who became more unpleasant the more they drank. What brings you here so early in the morning?

She shouted as she spoke since Abundio was deaf.

—Just needing a cuartillo of alcohol.

—Has Refugio fainted again?

—She died on me, Madre Villa. Just last night, about eleven. Even though I sold my burros. Sold them all hoping she'd get better.

—I don't hear a thing you're saying! Or maybe you're not saying anything? What was that?

—I said I spent the night watching over my dead wife, my Refugio. She took her last breath last night.

—So that's why I thought I smelled death. You know I even told Gamaliel: "It smells like someone in town has died." But he didn't listen to me, seeing as he was too busy getting wasted looking after those visitors. And you know how he is when he gets drunk. He laughs at everything and won't pay attention to no one. But tell me, do you have people coming for the wake?

—No one, Madre Villa. That's why I need the booze, to take the pain away.

—You want it straight?

—Yes, Madre Villa. To get wasted good and fast. Hand it over quick. I'm in a hurry.

—Seeing it's you, I'll give you two deciliters for the price of one. But tell your dead wife I always liked her and ask her to keep me in mind when she gets to Heaven.

—I will, Madre Villa.

—Tell her before she gets all cold.

—I'll tell her. I know she's counting on you to say prayers for her as well. Let's just say she was heartbroken when she died because no one was there to give her last rites.

—You mean you didn't go looking for Father Rentería?

—I did. But they told me he was up in the hills.

—In what hills?

—Just up there somewhere. You know they're part of that uprising.

—You mean he's mixed up in that too? Lord help us, Abundio.

—Why should we care, Madre Villa? Don't mean a thing to us. Pour me the other one, but off the books since Gamaliel's so out of it.

—Just don't forget to ask Refugio to plead with God on my behalf, since I can use all the help I can get.

—Don't worry yourself. I'll tell her as soon as I get back. I'll even have her give me her word if that's what it takes for you to stop fretting.

—That's it, that's exactly what you should do. You know how women are. You've got to hound them to get things done on time.

Abundio Martínez left another twenty centavos on the counter.

—Give me that other cuartillo, Madre Villa. And if you want to add a little extra, well that's up to you. But I promise to drink this one at home with my dead wife, alongside my Cuca.

—Get going then, before my son gets up. He's always in a bad mood when he wakes up drunk. Be quick about it, and don't forget to give my message to your wife.

He was sneezing as he left the store since the alcohol was pure fire. But he had heard that's how you could get drunk most quickly, so he swallowed one swig after another, fanning his mouth with the edge of his shirt. He had planned on heading straight home, where Refugio was waiting for him, but he got confused and ended up following the road that led him out of town.

—Damiana! —Pedro Páramo called out—. Come and see what this man coming up the road wants.

Abundio kept approaching, stumbling along, bobbing his head, at times crawling on all fours. He felt the earth turning inside out, spinning him around and then casting him aside. He struggled to grab hold, but when he had the ground firmly in his hands it would take off again, until eventually he stood in front of a man sitting next to a door. That's when he stopped:

—Give me a bit of charity so I can bury my wife —he said.

Damiana Cisneros prayed: "Deliver us, O Lord, from the snares of the evil one." She pointed her hands toward Abundio and made the sign of the cross.

Abundio Martínez gazed at that woman, at the terror in her eyes, at the cross she was making right in front of him, and he shuddered. He wondered if the Devil might have followed him there. He turned to look, expecting to be confronted with some malevolent being. When he saw nothing, he repeated:

—I've come for a little something to help bury my wife.

The sun had reached as high as his back. An early morning sun, almost cold, distorted by the dust kicked up from the ground.

Pedro Páramo's face was buried beneath blankets, as if hiding from the light, as Damiana's screams grew in strength, cutting across the fields: "They're killing don Pedro!" Abundio Martínez could hear the woman screaming. He didn't know how to make her stop. He couldn't gather his thoughts. He imagined that people even a long way off must be able to hear the old woman's shouts. Perhaps even his wife could hear them since the racket was making his own ears ring, although he couldn't understand a word she was saying. He thought of his wife laid out on her bed, all alone, resting outside in the cool air of the patio, where he had taken her to slow the stench. His Cuca, who just yesterday had slept with him, still very much alive, frisky as a filly, nibbling at him and rubbing her nose against his. This was the same woman who had given him a tiny little son that died only moments after birth, supposedly because she was unwell: from the evil eye, the chills, dyspepsia, or any number of other maladies, so said the doctor who came to see her at the last minute, but only after Abundio was forced to sell his burros on account of how much he charged. But it was all for nothing . . . His Cuca, who was now stretched out and covered in dew, her eyes closed tight, unable to watch this sunrise or any to come.

—Help me! —he said—. Give me a little something.

But even he couldn't hear his own words. The woman's screams were deafening.

A few black dots approached along the road from Comala. Soon those dots had turned into men, and then they were here, standing at his side. Damiana Cisneros stopped screaming. She stopped making the sign of the cross. She had fallen to the ground, her mouth open, as if she were yawning.

The men who had arrived lifted her off the ground and carried her into the house.

—Are you all right, patrón? —they asked.

Pedro Páramo's face appeared, but all he did was shake his head.

They disarmed Abundio, who still had the bloodied knife in his hand:

—Come with us —they told him—. You've gotten yourself into quite the mess.

And he followed.

Before getting to town, he asked to be excused. He moved to the side of the road and vomited out a yellowish substance, something like bile. Lots and lots of it, as if he had guzzled ten liters of water. After that his head began to burn and his tongue felt swollen:

—I'm drunk —he said.

He returned to where the men were waiting for him. He leaned on their shoulders, and they dragged him along, opening a furrow in the ground with the tips of his feet.

BEHIND THEM, STILL SITTING in his equipal, Pedro Páramo watched as the procession made its way toward town. As he tried to get up, he felt his left hand fall lifeless to his knees, but he thought nothing of it. He was accustomed to seeing a new part of his body die with each passing day. He watched as the paradise tree trembled, shaking off its leaves. "They all choose the same path. They all leave." Then he returned to the place where he had left his thoughts.

—Susana —he said. He closed his eyes—. I asked you to come back . . .

». . . An immense moon hung over the world. I stared at you until my vision seemed to fade. The rays of the moon filtering down on your face. I never grew tired of watching the apparition that you were. Soft, caressed by the moonlight. Your lips swollen, moist, shimmering with the stars. Your body growing translucent in the water of the night. Susana, Susana San Juan.»

He tried to raise his hand to reinforce the image in his mind, but his hand, heavy as if made of stone, would not lift off his legs. He tried to raise his other hand, but it dropped slowly down his side until it rested on the ground, like a crutch providing support for a shoulder that had gone limp.

«This is my death,» he said.

The sun began to cascade over all the things covering the earth, giving them back their shape. The land spread out before him, empty and in ruins. The heat warmed his body. His eyes barely moved, but they jumped from one memory to another, obscuring the present. Suddenly his heart stopped, and it seemed as if time as well had come to an end. And the breath of life with it.

«As long as this is not just another night,» he thought.

He dreaded the nights that filled the darkness with ghosts. That locked him in with his phantoms. That's what he feared.

«I'm sure Abundio will be back within a few hours with his blood-soaked hands to ask again for the help I refused him. And my hands won't be able to shield my eyes to keep from seeing him. I'll be forced to listen to him until his voice fades with the light of day, until his voice dies out.»

He felt hands on his shoulders, and he straightened up, becoming stiff.

—It's me, don Pedro —said Damiana—. Would you like me to bring out your breakfast?

Pedro Páramo replied:

—I'm coming. I'm coming now.

He supported himself on Damiana Cisneros's arms and tried to walk. After a few steps he fell, pleading on the inside, but without saying a word. He hit the ground with a hollow thud, crumbling as if he were a pile of rocks.

. . . .

TRANSLATOR'S NOTE

Douglas J. Weatherford

Since it first appeared in March of 1955, *Pedro Páramo* has always defied easy readings. Almost seven decades later, it is clear just how much this single work altered the course of Mexican and Latin American literature. Often considered Mexico's most significant novel, it is also the country's most translated work of fiction. *Pedro Páramo* has appeared in print in English twice before (translated by Lysander Kemp, 1959, and Margaret Sayers Peden, 1994, both from Grove Press). I am honored to offer this new translation that builds upon those earlier attempts to make Juan Rulfo's masterful narrative talents available to English-speaking readers.

This most recent rendition of *Pedro Páramo* is based on the definitive Spanish-language version that the Fundación Juan Rulfo and Editorial RM released in 2010. Many of the adjustments included in that updated edition were associated with the author's notable use of punctuation. In *Pedro Páramo*, Rulfo employs a variety of options to indicate dialogue: dashes (—), double (" ") and single (' ') quotation marks, guillemets or French quotation marks (« »), as well as italics. This range of punctuation is essential to Rulfo's narrative vision and adds one more level of complexity—although subtle—to a novel already designed to challenge its readers. English-language publications typically avoid both dashes and guillemets, however, and the previous versions of *Pedro Páramo* in that language deferred to such practice by removing both. The decision to precisely follow in this edition the author's original mode of punctuating dialogue reveals an immediate deviation from earlier versions of this iconic novel. Nonetheless, it is my belief that readers will discover numerous ways beyond issues of punctuation in which this newest translation of *Pedro Páramo* helps animate a novel that deserves a wider audience in the English-speaking world.

Ultimately, the desire to reflect more accurately both the letter and the spirit of Rulfo's fictional universe was fundamental in my efforts to translate one of the foundational novels of Latin America. Translation is not a trouble-free activity, however, and even the most reverential approach requires the translator to apply some level of force to an original text to fashion a work that will connect with a new audience that reads with different linguistic and cultural eyes. Although I am happy to leave the responsibility of evaluating my efforts to the reader, I offer here a sampling of the strategies that guided my labor.

"What Exactly Do You Understand?": The Challenge of *Pedro Páramo*

Nearing the halfway point of Juan Rulfo's groundbreaking novel, an incestuous brother and sister interrogate Pedro Páramo's estranged son with an inquiry that seems, in a metafictional masterstroke, to lift off the page and challenge the readers themselves: "What exactly do you understand?" *Pedro Páramo* is a novel that defies comprehension, with confusion and fragmentation becoming central to Rulfo's unstable fictional world. The novel vacillates between presence and absence, between reality and irreality, and even between life and death. It is my opinion that a successful translation of *Pedro Páramo* must honor Rulfo's deliberately fractured narrative and avoid the temptation to clarify complexities that are integral elements of the text, including the beautifully complicated use of punctuation mentioned above. From a stylistic perspective, I would like to highlight two tendencies of the narrative design of *Pedro Páramo*: a persistent use of syntactic constructions based on sentence fragments as well as an enthusiasm for the subjunctive mood. Rulfo's frequent reliance on sentence fragments helps establish the laconic or even staccato style for which the author is known. These verbless sentences echo the sense of disintegration and bewilderment found throughout the novel. Although a careful analysis of this translation will find some places where I added a verb to improve flow in English, my desire when confronting Rulfo's narrative was to reflect the volatile nature of both the author's style and storyline. As such, I also avoided the modern English tendency of minimizing the subjunctive mood. Throughout *Pedro Páramo*, Rulfo's characters as well as his largely absent third-person narrator typically eschew certainty when speaking. Similes abound in the novel, as do subjunctive constructions, for instance in this moment when Pedro Páramo's estranged son tries to make sense of the place where he has just arrived: "—No, I was asking about the town. It *seems* so alone, *as if* abandoned. *As if no one were* living here" (Page 5, emphasis mine). Although the overwhelming presence of the subjunctive throughout *Pedro Páramo* might feel unnatural to English-language readers, the mood is essential to the tone and texture of the novel, and I made every effort to preserve the hesitation that the use of this grammatical construction suggests.

There are other elements of Rulfo's narrative vision that are more difficult to preserve, including the author's use of regional vocabulary. Rulfo was known for his fascination with the distinctive language heard throughout the rural communities of his home state of Jalisco. He was particularly captivated by archaic terms that survived from the earliest periods of Spanish colonization, as well as by ones inherited from Indigenous languages in a region of Mexico where most native communities disappeared through violence or assimilation. It is simply too difficult to retain many of Rulfo's lexical flourishes in any natural way in translation. Nonetheless, the reader of this translation will notice a variety of words (e.g., turicata) that display Rulfo's semantic flair, especially when it seemed clear that these words would prove equally strange for Spanish- and English-language readers. Finally, I should point out that Rulfo, despite his interest in Mexico's linguistic variation, used colloquial language only sparingly, and its general absence in my translation is true to the original.

Although *Pedro Páramo* presents both the reader and the translator with many other demands, the final ones I will mention here relate to an allusive richness of the text that is at once historical and mythical. Rulfo places the action of his novel during a momentous period of Mexican history that begins during the dictatorship of Porfirio Díaz (1876–1911), continues through the Mexican Revolution (1910–1917), and concludes sometime after the Cristero Revolt (1926–1929). This historical context is crucial to Rulfo's narrative vision and yet may be unfamiliar to many readers outside of Mexico. As would become the hallmark of the experimental writers of the so-called Latin American Boom movement who would follow in his footsteps (including Nobel laureates Gabriel García Márquez and Mario Vargas Llosa), Rulfo offers only limited expository assistance. Instead, Rulfo's narrative is defined by a faith in the ability of diligent readers to discover the interpretive possibilities hidden within the disintegration of his novel. And the richness of *Pedro Páramo* goes well beyond Rulfo's desire to depict the sociohistorical reality of a Mexican town dominated by an abusive cacique. Indeed, the novel overflows with poetic possibilities. Sound is vital, as is silence. Upward and downward movements carry semantic weight, symbols and analogies abound, and the text is built on archetypal underpinnings that constantly reward the thoughtful bibliophile. Faced with such a rich fictional source, I saw my responsibility as translator to safeguard—but not to lay bare—the abundance of connotations embedded within Rulfo's masterpiece. I am aware, however, that there are times when such an approach may leave diligent readers of *Pedro Páramo* in translation at a disadvantage. For example, Rulfo chose names that function as literary analogies for many of his characters and the places they inhabit. Although the deeper significance of these labels (e.g., Comala suggests the heat associated with the traditional comal used for warming tortillas while Pedro Páramo's first name alludes to the biblical Peter and his last to the Spanish word for "wasteland") is veiled whether one reads the novel in the original language or in translation, speakers of Spanish are more likely to discern their deeper meanings. I encourage all to approach Juan Rulfo as active rather than passive readers, willing to accept the challenge offered by the incestuous brother and sister who ask: "What exactly do you understand?"

Pedro Páramo is a treasure of the Mexican and Latin American literary landscapes, and it has been my pleasure to render the novel into a new English translation. I offer my sincere gratitude for this opportunity to the Fundación Juan Rulfo and to the entire Rulfo family. I am inspired by their commitment to protect and disseminate the artistic legacy of one of the greatest writers of the twentieth century. In particular, I would like to acknowledge Víctor Jiménez, tireless director of the Fundación Juan Rulfo, who spent significant time—in person and via email—responding to my persistent inquiries. I also thank Peter Blackstock of Grove Atlantic, Leonora Craig Cohen of Serpent's Tail, and my wife, Terri, for their enthusiastic support for this project and for their careful reading of my translation.